Sunflower

A NOVEL

Francis Eugene Wood

Published by Tip-of-the-Moon Publishing Company
Farmville, Virginia

Printed by Farmville Printing
Photo of author by Daniel Wood
Back cover photo by FEW

Book design by the author and Jon Marken

First USA Printing

Email address: fewwords@moonstar.com
Website: www.tipofthemoon.com
Or write to: Tip-of-the-Moon Publishing Company
175 Crescent Road, Farmville, Virginia 23901

ISBN: 0-9746372-9-7

Acknowledgments

Thanks to my wife, Chris, for her patience and encouragement in bringing this story to the bookshelf. Thanks to Jon Marken for his sharp editing skills and advice. It is always a joy to work with Dan Dwyer and the staff at Farmville Printing. I am honored that Eldridge Bagley has created another fine original painting to grace the cover of this book, and that Martha Pennington Louis has produced the illustrations that serve to divide the passages. I am thankful for the things I cannot explain—the lone dove that came into my yard during the entire writing of this story, and the butterflies that appeared, out of season, at my study window, and those that fluttered above the pages as I wrote from my chair on the deck of my cabin in the woods. I am thankful for the beauty of a sunflower field and for the gentle spirit of the young man who inspired this story.

Dedication

In memory of Billy C. Clark
December 29, 1928 – March 15, 2009

Friend and mentor

Preface

The Discovery

Years have passed, but, even now, my memory of that day has not diminished. I can see it. I can feel it. The wind on my face, and the sun warm on my hands. That is how it began, with me and my youngest son driving along a winding country road. We explored unknown territories back then in my old Chevy truck. I called our excursions "little adventures." He was six years old. His head turned to the side as he peered out the window into deep hardwood forests he would not have dared to enter alone. Long shadows were mysterious to him. Unlike his older brother, this boy could not run through the woods. Forest floors offered uneven footing, and his sense of balance was delicate. But he liked to see things. And he loved to ride in vehicles.

I told the boy to keep his eyes open for something special as we crossed a narrow bridge and started up a long incline. A discovery. It might be a turtle on the road or a turkey at the edge of a field. Or, perhaps, the largest tree we had ever seen. I just did not know what we would find. Such was the lure of unfamiliar roads.

As we came to the top of the hill, I recall looking in the rearview mirror. The shadowed confinement of the road behind us seemed even darker. And then suddenly we drove out of the shadows and into a world of spectacular light. My son leaned forward and gripped the dashboard with his small fingers. The look on his face expressed the words he could not say. I immediately pulled the truck over to the side of the road, and we sat there in silent awe. A long minute passed before I opened the door and slid off my seat. "Let's stand on the back of the truck," I said as I swung into the truck's bed. My son scooted across the seat and climbed down onto the grassy roadside. He ran around to the rear of the truck and waited at the gate with his hands raised. I reached down and pulled him up. Then I lifted him onto the roof of the truck's cab. Together we took in the beauty of our discovery. "Sunflowers," I said. "Aren't they amazing?"

The boy did not answer. Instead, he smiled and looked around. The fields on both sides of the road were like mirrors of the sun. The warm afternoon breeze tilted the towering flower heads as if they were nodding giants. Bees and butterflies flitted among them and hovered over them. A bluebird lit upon the seeded brown face of a flower close to us and left it swaying back and forth. The little bird flew over our heads, his beak ajar with a dark seed. I do not know how long we stayed there, bedazzled by the beauty of the flower fields. I do recall that no one passed by us during that time. And that, somehow, made our discovery even more special.

I told my son that the sunflowers were called mammoths and that they would grow very tall. At that time, they were perhaps seven to eight feet in height. We saw lots of animal tracks. I mentioned that bears liked to eat sunflower seeds. The boy's eyes grew large, and I knew he was hoping that I was just teasing him. He wanted to walk beneath the towering flowers, so we did for a little while. It was a good adventure. Before we left, we made a father and son pact that we would never forget our great discovery and our walk in the sunflower field. We looked intently at the beautiful flowers, then closed our eyes tightly and waited as their impression drifted across the darkness of our eyelids.

That night, as my son played with his toy cars on the den floor, the news that aired over the television was somber, even troubling. I noticed that, occasionally, he would look up at the screen, and I knew that he was listening to every word. There was not a happy or inspiring story during the entire newscast. Finally, I turned off the television and called the boy to come over to me. Quietly, he came and sat on the stone fire hearth beside my chair. He rolled a red toy fire engine across my knee and waited. This is what I said. "I know that you hear and see such bad stories every day. And I know that they frighten you and make you sad. But I want you to know that there is also much goodness in the world. And, one day, that goodness will prevail. God will shine his light on the hearts of men everywhere, and they will open up to him. Finally they will understand how to live in peace and harmony. There will be no wars and no hatred. No starving children. I have heard this all of my life. But words are cheap. So I want you to know that I believe this in my heart."

I did not expect my son to understand all of what I had said, nor did I expect him to say anything. His vocabulary was limited. Cerebral palsy will do that.

He rolled the little fire engine slowly over my knee again. Then suddenly he leaned forward and hugged me.

"Close your eyes and tell me what you see," I said. It was a game we sometimes played.

He closed his eyes and, after a moment, he said, "Sunflowers."

It was a word I had never heard him say. It was plain and simple and yet, for some reason, it meant everything to me. It still does. I have never forgotten that day. The beauty of that sunflower field remains locked in my memory. And the word my son spoke still echoes along the corridors of my mind.

For a long time now I have had recurring dreams of that sunflower field. Lately, the dreams have come more frequently. I do not doubt that there is a reason for it. To tell you that I see sunflowers in my sleep is an understatement. I see them everywhere—no matter where I am. There is a purpose in that. I know it.

So now I give you a story that began a long time ago on a sunny afternoon in the country. It is a gift I found in the brilliance of a sunflower field and the vision of a little boy.

A Walk to the Cedar Swing
(A day some time in the future)

The morning sun pressed the clouds that hovered above the rolling hills as the woman walked along the narrow well-kept road that led into the village. Cassidy paused at the crest of a hill. She set down her straw bag and adjusted her wide-brimmed hat. Her gnarled fingers felt tight, but they did not pain her. She stretched them and placed her hands on her hips. A flock of blackbirds lifted from the canopy of a massive oak tree in the field beside her. The birds descended the hill just above the treetops like a fast-moving black cloud. Cassidy watched as the birds suddenly turned sharply in unison and fell into the shadowy foliage of a cluster of hardwoods.

The forest was awakening. She could hear the songs of birds as they greeted the day. A bumblebee passed sluggishly by her face. Cassidy reached up with her hand as if to touch the bee. "My hat is yellow, but it's no flower, Buzzy," she said. The bumblebee dodged her uplifted hand and rose higher until it was out of sight.

The woman's lively brown eyes searched the sky. The clouds reminded her of an old worn quilt, ragged at its edges and thin in patches. In a minute, its seams tore loose, and the sun reached its finger-like rays into the lush green foliage of the trees and the rolling landscape that cradled the village of Hopeful.

Cassidy folded her arms beneath her breasts. The sunlight found her face, and she closed her eyes and felt its warmth. There was light behind her eyelids. She inhaled the freshness of the cool morning air that lifted out of the hollows. She could hear the gurgle of a nearby stream that pooled beneath the sycamores and fell along slick and mossy crevices.

Cassidy opened her eyes. A feeling of reverie swept over her. A wanting in her heart. She felt a sudden desire to dash into the woods and follow the stream. She longed to meander along its banks as she had as a child. She wanted to look up and see the sunlight streaming down through the leaves of the trees. She wanted to sink her hands into the pools of water and feel the cool, thick mud between her fingers. Those memories were dear to her heart. For a moment, she was not aware of the arthritis in her joints. For a moment, she was young again. "Hopeful," she said softly. "My good little town," she whispered. The quaint village was coming to life. Cassidy could see the main street that stretched from east to west and the avenues and narrow alleys. A dog barked in the distance, and she watched as Mr. Scott began his morning deliveries in his horse-drawn milk wagon. The old milkman made several deliveries on Main Street and then turned his wagon and disappeared into a fold in the hills. The Jarrells, Postons, and Abrams lived back there. Cassidy knew the families well. The church steeple shone brilliantly in the morning sunlight. She recalled as a young girl three other churches in the community. But that was long ago. Now there was only one, standing tall in the center of the village. Everyone went there. There was no separation among Christians. There were no denominations and no need for them.

Cassidy picked up her bag and followed the road into Hopeful. She liked the tidiness of the houses and the neatly kept yards. Everything was sharp and bright.

Rebecca Sterling paused from sweeping her front porch and greeted Cassidy as she passed by her picket fence. "Good morning, Cass," the smiling woman called.

"Good morning, Rebecca." Cassidy slowed her pace as she spoke.

"How is Daniel?" The woman leaned on her broom handle as she posed her question.

Cassidy paused and glanced up at the hill ahead of her. She could see the house perched atop it. She looked back at the woman on the porch. "He's doing as well as possible. You know him. Every day now is a diamond."

Rebecca smiled. She had heard Daniel say that on many occasions. "Well, you tell him Jack and I will come up soon and bring him some Amish bread."

"Oh, he'll love that," Cassidy nodded her head, "and the visit, too."

Rebecca waved and stepped back into her house.

Cassidy knew and loved the people of Hopeful. They were good and kind folks, who really cared about each another. It was one of the reasons Cassidy had come back there to live after the passing of her husband. And, of course, there was Daniel. Daniel, who knew and cared for everyone, and who, in turn, was loved and cherished by all. He was a great part of what had made Hopeful the place it was. Cassidy knew that. But she did not know everything. Only that something had happened there that few people could remember. It was so long ago that only Daniel, the ancient old man who lived on the hill overlooking the village, could recall it. But Daniel was quiet and unable to tell a very detailed account. It was perhaps a bit odd that as close as Cassidy was to him, she did not know the facts surrounding his stature among the people of Hopeful. In the seven years since she had come back to live there and care for him, she had gotten but one word from Daniel whenever she asked about the town's past. One word. But she knew that in that word lay the answer she desired. *Someday*, she thought. Someday she would know. Someday he would tell her. But Daniel's days were now diamonds. He was so old. No one knew his age. There were no records left from the old days. Only some stories about how the world had become dark and evil in the last days before "the awakening." "The change."

By the time Cassidy stood at the edge of the vast flower garden that surrounded Daniel's house, the clouds had dissipated, and the sunlight had captured the rolling hillsides and the flats that separated the houses in the village below. Children were coming out of their homes to play. There was a bustle of activity along the main street. People filled the sidewalks and strode in and out of stores and shops. Vegetable gardens were being tended to, and farmers were heading into the fields.

Yes, there was truly something special about the town called Hopeful. Cassidy could feel it. But she could not explain it. For an instant, she was overcome with emotion and tears welled in her eyes. They were not tears of sadness, but ones that replace the words we cannot find to describe the things that humble us most. She wiped her eyes and turned toward the house. Daniel was expecting her, and she was so looking forward to his company.

"Good morning, Cassidy." Samantha Dandridge, a plump, middle-aged woman with graying hair at her temples and a jovial disposition, pushed open the wide screen door and stepped to the side as Cassidy moved past her.

"Good morning, Sam." Cassidy lay her straw bag on the kitchen counter, unbuttoned the top button of her thin cotton blouse and dabbed her moistened neck with a small handkerchief she drew from her skirt pocket. The walk up the hill to the house had exhausted her. She leaned against the counter as Samantha closed the screen door and faced her. "Are you all right, dear?" The younger woman walked over to the kitchen sink and filled a small glass with well water from a pail positioned beside the sink. She handed it to Cassidy and pulled a chair over for her to sit on.

"Thank you, Sam." Cassidy sat down and took a sip of the cool water. "I'm fine. I guess I was just in too big a hurry to get up here this morning." She smiled and touched her lips with her handkerchief. "I usually pull that hill pretty well for an old woman."

"Why do you always walk up here? You know anybody would be happy to bring you." Samantha dried a cereal bowl and placed it atop others in a cabinet as she spoke. "You've been making that trek across town for a long time. Maybe it's best now we get someone to help you."

Cassidy shook her head and smiled. "Sam, it's my morning ritual. My exercise. And besides, I like to see the village come to life." She set her glass on the counter. "This morning, on my way here, I felt like a little girl again and had a strong yearning to skip along through the woods."

"You best be careful of that yearning. I'd hate to find you out there with a sprain, or worse." Samantha hung her dishtowel on a rack beside the sink and walked over to the bedroom door at the end of the counter. She peeked around the door. Then she reached down and picked up a small cloth overnight bag she had placed at the door's entrance. She pulled the long strap over her shoulder. "He's even more quiet than usual this morning." Samantha's voice was soft, as if the person in the next room were sleeping.

"How was his night?" Cassidy stood up and smoothed out her skirt with her hands.

"He fell asleep early last night. But this morning I heard him talking long before daylight."

"Oh?" Cassidy walked over and looked into the bedroom.

Daniel was sitting in a rocking chair that had been pulled over to the window overlooking the flower garden and the southern hillside. His face was turned toward the window.

Samantha put Cassidy's empty water glass next to the sink and walked over to the screen door. She pushed the door open, then motioned for Cassidy to step closer to her. "It was like he was talking to someone. I let it go on for a while before I got up from the table and walked in there. I found him fully dressed and sitting on the edge of the bed. He was wide awake and smiled at me when he saw me. All that talking, and he was there all alone." Samantha shook her head thoughtfully. "I asked him why he was up and dressed so early, and all he said was that it was a special day. He wanted to go out and sit on the swing, but he could hardly make it over to the window."

"Has he had anything to eat this morning?" Cassidy held the screen door open as she asked.

Samantha shook her head. "He wouldn't take nothin' but tea. Said he wasn't hungry."

Cassidy looked behind her, then back at Samantha. "I'll see if I can get him to eat a little, Sam."

"Thanks for stayin' through tonight, Cassidy." Samantha turned to leave. "I'll see you tomorrow morning."

Cassidy smiled and closed the screen door. "You enjoy your night at home, Sam. We'll be fine." She watched Samantha walk away. Then she turned around. The house was quiet. She opened her straw bag and brought out two small jars of strawberry preserves. Daniel loved the delicious treat spread over two steaming, buttered biscuit halves. She carried the bag with her out of the kitchen and through the living room to the bedroom at the front of the house. It was a small room with a window that looked out over the village. She pulled her nightgown and a few articles of clothing from the bag and laid them out on the small bed. There was no need to bring much with her for overnight stays, as the shallow closet in the room was filled with her own clothes and a couple of pairs of shoes. Her toiletries were in an adjoining bathroom. She pulled open an oak drawer and put her things away. Then she walked back into the kitchen. She rinsed and dried her water glass. The fluttering wings of a butterfly drew her attention to the window above the sink. She leaned toward it, her fingers touching the window panes. "A tiger swallowtail," she said in a whisper. Daniel had taught her how to identify the butterflies when she was a young girl. There was nothing scientific about his descriptions. He had simply called them by names his grandmother had taught him when he was a boy helping her in her flower gardens.

Cassidy walked to Daniel's bedroom door and looked across the room. The window curtains were open, and the morning sun doused the plaid blanket that Samantha had laid over his legs. It gave brilliance to the greens and reds, and radiance to the yellows in the weave. The swallowtail she had watched through the kitchen window was now fluttering its wings in the breeze outside Daniel's window. She noticed when Daniel raised his fingers toward the butterfly.

"It's a swallowtail, Daniel," she said softly as she touched his shoulder. "Remember? You taught me that when I was a little girl." She bent down and kissed the man on the forehead. Then she waved her hand, and the butterfly darted away toward a line of marigolds that dressed the edge of a stone wall. Daniel's grandfather had built the wall using field stone Daniel and he had gathered. Over the years, the yard around the house had become a maze of stone structures. The most colorful varieties of flowers were enclosed within those winding walls. There were tulips and daffodils, zinnias and black-eyed Susans. There were petunias, lilies and periwinkle. Multi-colored roses, hybrid teas and flora bundas graced stone corners and ran along split-railed fences. Blaze climbers groped at aged cedar rails, and evening primrose stood like shy boys at a school dance against the outer west wall of the board and batten house. There were long inviting walkways cloaked with wisteria, and terraces of periwinkle and ivy. A cedar porch swing hung from a beam between two thick posts on the highest terrace in the yard. It had been Daniel's favorite place to sit outside ever since Cassidy could remember, there above the gardens that he and his grandmother had planted and nurtured. From that vantage point he could sit and look out upon the fields and hillsides at the great swaying flowers that mirrored the sun.

Daniel looked up and smiled. "I remember," he said. "My little girl." He reached out his big hand and squeezed her fingers. "Good morning, Cass."

Cassidy pulled a straight-back wooden chair over and sat down. She carefully buttoned down the collar of his neatly-pressed white shirt. "There now," she said as she finished. "You are very handsome in your white shirt today, Daniel."

The old man smiled. "Thank you, Cass," he answered. He looked over at Cassidy for a moment and then back out the window. A comfortable silence followed. Minutes of thought and memories, unhindered by needless words. It was their ritual. A time when words were not important. Cassidy found peace in Daniel's presence. His love, a fatherly love, was more important to her than she could have explained. She had tried to tell him once how she felt. But halfway through it, he quieted her with one of his big hugs. "My little girl," he had said. He knew. She did not have to tell him. He seemed to have a gift for knowing one's heart.

"Samantha said you are not hungry this morning."

Daniel shook his head slowly.

"She said you told her it's a special day."

There was no immediate reaction from the man. Long minutes passed before he spoke. "The clouds are gone, Cass."

Cassidy leaned forward in her chair and looked up into the sky. "Yes, Daniel. The clouds have all gone away."

"The sun is coming into the fields." Daniel's speech was slow, with pauses between his words.

Cassidy looked past the yard at the rolling hillside where the great flowers swayed in the morning breeze. It reminded her of golden waves on an ocean. Their beauty was immeasurable. "What is it, Daniel?" There was a sincerity in Cassidy's question. A pleading from her heart. "What is it about the sunflowers?" She looked at the profile of his face. Age had not robbed him of his handsomeness. There were few creases in his olive skin, and he wore his grayness like a crown of wisdom. His brown eyes were still sharp and even penetrating. His lips, full and still. There was a reverence in his quiet nature. "The sun is coming into the field, Cass," he said as he turned and faced her. He could perceive her puzzlement. The story she wanted so desperately to know was in his mind. It was a story he had lived, and one her parents had witnessed. It would have flowed from his heart, if he had had the ability to form the words lodged inside of him.

But that day was a special day. Daniel knew it in his heart. And so he said the one word that could begin the story he could not tell. He parted his lips and touched his mouth with his fingers. "Sunflower" was the word he said. There was nothing more than that.

Cassidy closed her eyes. She knew he could not tell her what she wanted to know, and she felt a touch of guilt for pressuring him to go beyond his capability. But there are mysteries in this life we are not to understand. They surround us like the air we breathe. They tease us by touching our lives and avoiding our perception. God must have His mysteries, for how dull the world would be without them.

What Cassidy did not know was that when Daniel said the word, the breath of his soul spilled into the air like a whisper from angels and rode upon the breeze into the field of sun where it turned and swirled among the vibrant petals of the great towering flowers locked in their eastward gaze. Nature responded. The wind rose up and swept the whisper into a vortex that moved across the field unseen and dissipated at the edge of the yard beyond the cedar swing. A fluttering of wings opened Cassidy's eyes. "Oh, the swallowtail is back," she commented. She felt as if she had just awakened. The sound of wind chimes barely masked the soft squeak of the swing chains in the garden. For a moment, the butterfly came to rest on the petal of an orange day lily. Then suddenly it darted away toward the swing.

Cassidy stood up and bent toward the window to see where it would go. That is when she saw a man sitting in the swing. Startled, she turned to Daniel. "There's someone sitting in your swing, Daniel." Her voice was not loud. She looked again. "Were you expecting company?" she asked.

Daniel smiled. He did not look toward the swing. "Yes," he answered.

"Who is it?" Cassidy was intrigued.

"A friend." Daniel was the king of short answers.

"Does your friend have a name?"

Daniel looked up. Cassidy thought his brown eyes were as rich as the center of a black-eyed Susan. "He has a story, Cass."

Cassidy leaned over again and looked out the window at the stranger. "Sam told me that she heard you talking to someone earlier this morning." She turned her head and looked at Daniel. "Was it that man?"

Daniel did not answer her question. Instead, he reached out his hand and touched her forearm. "Go out and listen to the story, Cass. It's the one you want to know."

Cassidy did not question Daniel again, and a minute later she walked up the stone steps that led to the terrace above the flower garden. She stood at the top of the steps, intrigued by the sight of what seemed to be scores of butterflies. They fluttered about the man, alighting on his hat and shoulders as he pushed the swing gently back and forth with one foot on the ground. The fragrance of honeysuckle and lavender filled the air as Cassidy approached the man and walked around the swing to where she could see his face.

The butterflies lifted from the man's hat and shoulders when he looked up at her. "Hello, Cassidy. I have been waiting for you." The man smiled and tipped his short-brimmed straw hat as he offered his greeting.

"You know my name," Cassidy responded. There was no hint of astonishment in her voice. Somehow it did not even seem odd to her that this man would know her. A quick study told her that he was sincere. His blue eyes sparkled with life, captivating and wise. Gentleness emanated from his sun-tanned face. His skin lacked the ravage of age, and the hair at the edge of his temples was as white as a cloud. His posture was natural, his shoulders, level and broad. In a deep and soothing voice, he answered, "Yes. Daniel told me your name." The man rose, and a small-winged butterfly lit upon the brim of his hat. He raised his hand, and the butterfly transferred onto his forefinger. Then he reached out and offered the colorful creature to Cassidy.

Unsure, Cassidy put out her hand. She laughed aloud when the butterfly walked onto her finger. The man stepped to the side and motioned for Cassidy to sit beside him on the swing. "Ah. My little friend takes to you as if you were a flower in Daniel's garden."

Cassidy sat down. "I've never felt like a flower before now," she responded. She turned her head and looked into the man's eyes. His gaze drew her in. She felt as though her soul had immersed itself into a blue ocean. A feeling of lightness came over her. Trust. She wanted to know his name, but she did not have to ask.

"I am Isaac. Isaac Heartwell. I was a friend to Daniel before the world changed."

"Before?" Cassidy could not seem to remember.

"You did not know that world, Cassidy."

Cassidy shook her hand and watched the butterfly flutter away. She looked beyond Isaac, and for a moment she tried to recall a world other than the one she knew. "My mother and father knew it." She spoke as if lost in time. "But...."

Isaac finished her thought. "They spoke little of it."

Cassidy looked at Isaac and then out into the golden hills. For all of her life, she could never fully imagine the world they had known. "They said it had become dark and treacherous. They said that the people were cruel and hard-hearted. Kindness and respect for one's fellow man were not virtuous attributes. Wrong had become right, and right wrong." Cassidy stopped there. She did not know what else to say.

Isaac closed his eyes and glanced into the past. He winced and clinched his jaws. When he opened his eyes again, he nodded his head. "Your parents were wise, Cassidy. The world was as they told you. You see, the morality that was the basis for civilized men both in government and religion was compromised by greed. Selflessness was forgotten, and a curtain of darkness was drawn over the souls of men so that they could no longer see the light within them. Mistrust and hatred spread like cancers. War became a way of life. Man's faith in God was questioned by even the most devout believers. The curtain of darkness that shrouded their souls could not be lifted by the words and deeds of crafty politicians or by the promises of priests. No war or triumph could bring mankind out of the darkness that had settled over that world."

"But something did." Cassidy looked into Isaac's eyes as she interjected. "Something did occur that changed things forever."

Isaac smiled. "Yes. Something did occur. Something that was miraculous in the darkness of that world." Isaac breathed in the July morning. He had always loved the summers. And the garden. Daniel had kept it just the way his grandmother had. And when finally age prevented him from tending it, the people of Hopeful came and took over. They planted, raked and hoed. They cherished Mary Taylor's roses. They watered and mulched her colorful-petaled darlings. And they worked the fields where sunflowers stood like giant soldiers clad in gold.

"Daniel says the sun is coming into the field." Cassidy watched a pair of mourning doves descend into the shadows at the edge of the sunflower field at the end of the yard. "He has said it often when he looks out there."

Isaac looked at the woman but remained silent.

"What does he mean, Isaac?" Cassidy turned to the man with tears in her eyes. "He's my godfather. My parents loved him, and I have loved him all my life. He tells me things so simple, yet beautiful. But I don't understand. I want to understand."

Isaac felt compassion for the woman. He knew her heart was true. He reached over and patted her hand. "I came here to tell you the story that Daniel cannot tell." He placed his hat back on his head. "The answer to your question is in his story."

Cassidy wiped a tear from her cheek. Then she laid her hand over Isaac's. "Tell me. I want to know."

Isaac smiled, then settled back against the worn rails of the cedar swing. He pushed the swing back and forth with the toe of his shoe and began. "The story you desire is of a spiritual awakening that changed the world from what it was to what it is today. That awakening began here, just before you were born. Daniel was a young man then. There were no golden fields, and there were few smiling and friendly faces in the town. It was a different time. A different world when…."

SUNFLOWER
(The Planting of the Seeds)

Daniel closed the truck door and walked up the cobblestone path toward the back door of the house he shared with his grandmother. A stunted yellow rose too heavy for its stem lay like a sleeping dog, still and alone, on a split-cedar rail. Its red and yellow siblings bunched healthfully over it. Daniel paused and looked at the sad-looking rose. He lifted it, then let go. There was no support from its thin stem, and the rose fell back down on the splintered rail. The young man reached into his pants pocket and pulled out a small pocket knife his grandfather had given him for his fifteenth birthday. The knife was seven years old now, but Daniel kept its edge as sharp as the day he opened it. Carefully, he sliced the rose from its stem. He put his knife away and walked to the door. Once inside, he went into the kitchen, where he bent down and pulled open a cabinet door. After rummaging a bit, he brought out a small, thin-necked glass vase. He filled it with water from the faucet and placed the rose in it. *Mimi will like that*, he thought. *Where is she, anyway?* He looked out the window above the sink and saw his grandmother watering tulips in her flower garden. *My seeds*, he thought. He carried the rose vase with him as he hurried out of the kitchen door and back out to his truck, where he retrieved a small package he had brought from the village. He tucked the package in his back pocket and walked around to the south side of the house.

"Hi, Mimi." Daniel approached the woman with his hands behind his back.

Mary Taylor looked up from her chore and wiped the perspiration from her upper lip and chin with a handkerchief. "Well, you're home already?"

Daniel smiled and held out the rose for her.

"Oh, Daniel," she said in an excited tone. "You found that little sick rose and made it beautiful." She set down her watering can and took the vase from her grandson. "See how it looks so pretty in the vase." She put the vase down on the slate patio table and pulled out one of the chairs to sit in.

Daniel positioned the other chair and sat down. He looked at the yellow rose. "It was all alone, Mimi," he said. His words came slowly.

"I know it was," Mimi agreed. "But now we can treat it as though it is the prettiest rose from the garden."

Daniel smiled. "I got something, Mimi." He reached into his back pocket and brought out the package he had gotten in the mail.

"What is it?" Mary pulled off her gardening gloves and placed them on the table as she watched Daniel wrestle with the package. "Pull the little string there," she pointed, "and it will open."

Daniel found the string and pulled it. Seven shiny envelopes fell out on the table. "Sunflowers." Daniel pushed the envelopes to his grandmother. "I want to plant them."

Mary read the packages. "I haven't planted sunflowers in a long time," she said as she fanned out the envelopes. "You ordered these through the mail?"

"They were free," Daniel answered proudly. "If you sent four dollars." He took the envelopes from his grandmother and looked at the colorful pictures. "Can I plant them, Mimi?"

"Where?"

Daniel looked across the yard at an area where his grandfather used to have a vegetable garden. "Out there," he pointed.

Mary looked at the old garden site. It was covered with weeds. There had been no garden there since her husband had passed three years ago. It made her sad to look at the overgrown garden plot. But she did not have the strength to plant and work a garden. And Daniel had never shown an interest in having one of his own. "Why do you want to plant sunflowers, Daniel?" She was curious and always interested in the reasons behind his motivations.

"I dreamed about it."

"You dreamed about planting sunflowers?"

"Sunflower fields," Daniel corrected her. "All around us."

"Oh, you dreamed about sunflower fields." Mary lifted her eyebrows as she spoke. "Were they pretty?" she asked.

Daniel struggled for the word he wanted. "Beautiful," he finally managed.

"Well, you are going to have to till up the ground. I don't think it will be too difficult. The soil should be pretty soft, since we've had some rain lately. That dirt is rich, too."

Daniel stared out at the weedy site.

"Do you think you can do it?" Mary wondered at her grandson's ambition.

"Yes." His answer came without hesitation.

"You'll find your grandfather's tiller around back in the shed. Ned Johnson borrowed it last week to work up his little garden. He said the tiller was working fine. But it needs some gas, and the oil needs to be checked." Mary looked at the packages her grandson had ordered. "You've got a good variety of miniatures here, and I like the Mexican Thithonia." She separated the mammoth sunflower seed packets from the rest. "My goodness, Daniel, you sure ordered enough of the big ones to plant."

Daniel watched his grandmother separate the seed packets. He smiled. "I know, Mimi. They will grow tall, like I saw in my dreams."

Mary reached across the table and touched Daniel's hand as he tried to make sense of the planting instructions. "You just plow up the garden, and I'll tell you how to plant the seeds." She squeezed his hand. "This is important to you, isn't it?"

Daniel smiled, his dark brown eyes intent upon the garden area. He did not have to answer his grandmother. She knew him well. His passions ran deep, and when he set his mind on a goal, he did not lag in his pursuit of attaining it.

Daniel was a unique young man. The cerebral palsy that robbed him of what most people would call a normal existence had, in fact, served to shelter him from some of the harshness of the world. There was such goodness in him. He had an ability to forgive the cruelties cast upon him by those who did not understand him. He was quiet and observant and capable of so much more than anyone but he could have imagined. There was power in his presence. Children and old people recognized it. They did not take advantage of the innocence that left Daniel vulnerable to those who would try to deceive him. Daniel did not deserve the world he was born into. But the world deserved him.

Mary looked up at Daniel with pride as he stood up and spoke. "I'm going to till the garden now." His tongue struggled with the "t" in "till."

Mary watched him as he walked away, his tall, slender frame bent slightly forward. Few people would have noticed his lumbering gate. His physical appearance gave little indication of the frustrations of his mind and the limitations of his body. A timid silence masked the determination in him that had mystified the doctors who had said he would not be able to run or ride a bike or even tie his own shoelaces. Mary had seen him defy them all. But she was also afraid that one day the world he wanted so to be a part of would devour him. She worried. It was her nature. She thought that she was all he had. *What will Daniel do when I'm no longer here?* Oh, if Mary had only known that his life was special, even beyond the ways that she knew. For every good thing she had ever told Daniel was harbored within his heart. And the one thing she had not yet told him would be the final key to the purpose of his life.

Mary stood up. Her fingers ached from the arthritis that disfigured them. She thought beyond her pain, and in her mind she could imagine the garden bright with Daniel's sunflowers. The day was good, as she picked up her watering can and continued her task.

In the days that followed, Daniel toiled in the garden. He tilled the soil until it was loose. When he had finished, he went out into the fields around the house and tilled long swaths of soil where his grandfather had grown corn. He even tilled the ground around the borders in Mary's flower gardens, where he dropped the miniature sunflower seeds and the Mexican Thithonia. The mammoth sunflower seeds were for the garden lot and the fields. There, Daniel was careful to plant the seeds according to his grandmother's directions, three feet apart, in rows four feet apart. By the end of the first week in May, he had planted all of his seeds.

"What are you going to do now, Daniel?" Rosie Holman asked as she set a glass of ice water on the fence that enclosed the garden lot. Rosie was a heavy-set woman who came in weekdays to cook and tidy up the house for Mary. Daniel had known her all his life and thought of her as family.

"Thank you, Rosie." Daniel took a sip of the water and leaned his back against a fence post.

"I've never seen you work so hard at somethin'." Rosie was impressed. "Your granddaddy sure woulda' been proud of you. Your Mimi is."

"Did I get any mail today, Rosie?" Daniel wiped beads of perspiration from his forehead with the palm of his hand.

The big woman smiled. "There's a package layin' up there on the patio table with your name on it." She watched the smile creep across Daniel's lips. "I guess you ain't finished yet."

Daniel walked around the fence and hugged the woman. "I'm going to need the tractor."

Rosie turned toward the house. "Well, you best get Ned Johnson over here, 'cause your Mimi ain't gonna let you drive no tractor. You ain't never driven no tractor." Rosie waved her hand in the air.

Daniel fell in behind her. "Well, I'm going to," he said defiantly.

Rosie turned her head to the side as she continued walking. "You best take that up with your Mimi, Daniel. I'm gonna stay out of that one."

Clouds were gathering over Hopeful when Daniel pulled his truck into a parking space in front of Meek's Feed and Seed Store. He cut off the engine just as fat raindrops began decorating the truck's dusty hood with maroon polka dots. Daniel stepped out of the truck that had belonged to his grandfather and hurried to the front door of the store.

A bell rang as he entered. The scent of fertilizer stung his nostrils as he walked inside. John Grayling stepped to the side as Daniel moved past him. "Well, good mornin', Daniel." The old man smelled of pipe tobacco. Daniel liked the aroma.

"Hi." Daniel stopped and turned.

"How's your grandma?" John was holding the door open.

"Fine." Daniel smiled.

"That's good. You tell her howdy for me." John stepped out the door before Daniel said, "Okay."

When Daniel turned around, he almost walked into a young man he did not know. The man was carrying a bag of dog food under his arm when he stopped abruptly. "Hey. Watch it!" His voice was terse.

Daniel wanted to say "excuse me," but he could only manage "sorry." He rode the "s" for a few seconds before he got the word out.

The grungy stranger raised his eyebrows and

shot a glance over to a companion in the time it took to respond, "Yeah, whatever." The man snickered. "C'mon." He brushed by Daniel as he walked out the front door, followed by his scruffy companion.

"Don't mind them, Daniel." Forrest Meeks spoke from behind the counter. He leaned forward as Daniel approached him. "Those two aren't worth the worry they bring. The Scaggs brothers."

Daniel reached into his shirt pocket and unfolded a small piece of paper with his grandmother's handwriting on it. He gave it to the store owner. "Hi, Forrest."

Forrest held the piece of paper at arm's length and squinted his eyes. "Let's see, Daniel. What do you need today?" He read the list. "Fertilizer, phosphorous and potassium." He looked at Daniel. "Is that it?"

Daniel nodded his head. He did not look up. His eyes were intent upon the colorful seed packets that aligned a display tray on the counter. He could not make out all of the varieties of seeds, but he recognized the word "sunflower" at the top of each packet. He picked one up and handed it to Forrest.

The middle-aged man took the packet and read it. "Sunflowers." He looked at Daniel over the reading glasses he had pulled from his shirt pocket and propped on his nose. "I'll bet your grandma would love these, Daniel." He turned the packet over and read, "Summer Evening. Deep reds, golds and burgundies. Eight-inch flowers." Forrest chuckled, "Gracious, Daniel. These sunflowers can grow six to seven feet tall."

"What are these?" Daniel handed the man four other packets, all with the word "sunflower" at the top.

"Well, you've got Lemon Queen, a hybrid mix, and these here are the big mammoths." Forrest placed the seed packets down on the counter. He took off his glasses. "I've seen those mammoths grow over twelve feet tall."

"Where?" Daniel was curious.

"Bill and Hilda Burke over in Wayland County grew some of the big ones there." He touched the mammoth seed packet with his finger. "They actually harvested the flowers for the seeds and oil. Had a pretty good thing going for a while, until they just grew too old for the work. Their children didn't want to have anything to do with farming." Forrest shook his head. "Bill died, and Hilda got put away in a rest home. The kids sold the farm. Nobody around here that I know of has grown sunflowers for anything more than a flower garden for years." Forrest pursed his lips. "Shoot, Daniel, come to think of it, besides your grandma, there ain't even many folks out there wanting to keep up a flower garden any more. I don't sell nearly as many flower seeds as I used to. It's like folks these days don't have the desire to put some color in the world."

Daniel reached over and pushed the Lemon Queens and hybrid mix packets toward the store owner. He nodded at the Mammoth seed packet Forrest had touched. "I want to buy all of these you have."

Forrest was surprised. He looked at the face of the

young man standing at his counter. He had known Daniel since the days when the boy would ride along with his grandfather, Frank Taylor. A big man, Frank had worked for the power company for years before he retired to a life as a gentleman farmer. Everyone knew him. He was well respected, a quiet man who did more for others than anyone knew. Frank and Mary, his wife, had raised a son, Steven. Forrest had known the boy. They had played together as children in school. Steven Taylor was handsome, a good athlete, and well-liked—everything a parent could desire in a child. A sensitive type, Steven was troubled by the course of the world around him. After his graduation from high school, he enlisted in the military. He was killed in a quickly forgotten war. A year or so after his death, a baby boy was abandoned under a pink dogwood tree in Frank and Mary Taylor's back yard. They named him Daniel.

Forrest Meeks marveled at how much the young man resembled Steven Taylor. And although neither he nor anyone else in Hopeful knew the entire story of where Daniel had come from, everyone knew that Frank and Mary Taylor had raised him as if he were their own son. It could not have been easy for the aging couple, for the child had challenges. But they worked with him and gave him all the advantages they could. They treated him as one would treat a normal child, while knowing fully that he was a special gift to them. Mostly, they gave him the love and attention that he seemed to desire above anything else.

Forrest pulled the display stand around and collected all of the mammoth sunflower-seed packets he could find. He counted them. "With the two here on the counter, Daniel, you've got eighteen packets of seeds." Forrest arranged the packets on the counter.

"How many flowers is that?" Daniel struggled with his question.

"Well, let's see." Forrest rubbed his cheek with his thumb. "If you have about sixty seeds in each packet, that'll come to approximately"— he pressed the numbers into his calculator and touched the equal button—"one thousand eighty." He pushed the calculator toward Daniel and turned it around so that the young man could see the number.

Daniel stared at the calculator screen for a moment. "Can you order more?" he asked.

Forrest studied the look on Daniel's face. "How many do you want, Daniel?" He could sense the seriousness in the young man's question. He waited patiently for Daniel to answer.

"Fifty pounds."

"Where are you planning to plant all of these sunflowers?" Forrest tried to mask his surprise.

Daniel looked up at the ceiling as if the words he needed were drifting over his head.

Forrest knew Daniel's difficulty with words and waited without staring.

Finally, Daniel continued. "I have already planted some in my papa's garden. I want to plant these in the field all the way back to the woods."

Forrest visualized the Taylor place. "You mean, above the surface pond?"

Daniel nodded his head.

"That's a lot of ground, Daniel." Forrest knew that field. He had helped Steven pick corn there when they were boys. "You can't just drop these seeds down and expect them to grow. The birds will pick them up."

"I planted them in the garden already," Daniel offered.

"Who worked it up for you?" Forrest knew the old garden area had not been used since Frank's death.

"I did," Daniel answered with a hint of pride.

"You used your grandpa's tiller?" Forrest was surprised. He knew that Daniel was strong, but he had never imagined him using any kind of machinery. Obviously, there were things about Daniel Taylor he did not know.

Daniel nodded his head. "I have a tractor, too."

"Have you ever used the tractor, Daniel?"

"Not yet," Daniel said as he reached in his back pocket for his wallet. He opened the worn leather wallet that used to belong to his grandfather and laid two twenty-dollar bills on the counter. He looked at Forrest as if to ask if that was enough money.

Forrest worked up the charge with his calculator. "Okay, Daniel, that's a hundred pounds of fertilizer and two fifty-pound bags of phosphorous and potassium, and eighteen packets of sunflower seeds."

Daniel saw that Forrest had not put the two seed packets for his grandmother with the others. He reached over and pushed them toward the stack. "Those are free." The man smiled.

"Thank you." Daniel held his wallet in his hand

and waited for the sound on Forrest's calculator that would show him his charge.

"That'll be forty-two even, Daniel." Forrest took the two twenties as Daniel laid two one-dollar bills on the counter.

The store owner placed the seed packets in a brown bag and gave Daniel a yellow slip of paper. "Just pull around to the side and give this to Billy. He'll load you up in a jiffy. I'll call you when the other seeds come in."

Daniel took the bag and the slip of paper. "Thank you," he smiled.

"There's enough seed there to put some color in that field, Daniel. You be careful about that tractor, son. If you've never used it, you get Mary to give me a call. I'll get someone up there to lend you a hand."

Daniel smiled, but the conversation was over. He turned and walked out the front door.

Forrest watched Daniel get into his truck. He shook his head and thought, *nobody would've guessed that boy would ever drive a vehicle.* There were a lot of unknowns when it came to figuring Daniel.

Forrest turned up the volume on a small-screen television he kept on the shelf behind the counter. A crowd of mourners was holding up the body of a dead child. They were surrounded by the remains of a bombed-out town. Forrest shook his head as he stared at the tragedy. For a moment, he felt a pang of guilt for what he thought was his lack of compassion. He heard a reporter talking, but he did not really listen to what the man was saying. His emotion toward the state of the world seemed numb. Like so many others, he had become almost immune to the crumbling of society. The door of his feed and seed store and the picket fence at home kept the world at bay. "God," he whispered in disgust as he turned off the television. "The world is falling apart." He closed his eyes, but he could not rid his mind of the vision of the dead child on the news. There was still something deep within the soul of Forrest Meeks that would not allow his conscience to let go of his humanity. But the world seemed bleak, and the hope for change was like a dimming light in a dark and ominous forest. He believed that he had given up on the world. He thought that he had lost hope in mankind. Forrest often felt alone and helpless, even afraid.

Forrest heard the low rumbling of Frank Taylor's old truck, and suddenly he wanted to know something. He pushed away from the counter and hurried to the front door. Daniel had put the truck in reverse and was about to back up when he noticed the front door of the store open and Forrest come walking out. He rolled down his window and waited for the man to approach him.

"Why sunflowers, Daniel?" Forrest posed his question with his hands in his pockets. "Your grandpa always planted corn in that field."

Daniel opened his mouth and struggled with his first word. "I...had a dream."

"You had a dream?"

Daniel nodded his head.

For some reason, Forrest wanted desperately to

know about Daniel's dream. He wanted to know what would inspire the young man to pursue such a task. But he knew it was not his business to pry, so he did not ask any more questions. "Well, dreams are important, Daniel."

He stepped away from the truck and watched Daniel back up and pull around to the side of the store. A customer drove up, and Forrest straightened a display of garden rakes and shovels beside the front door. Then he went inside.

Billy Meeks was amazed at the ease with which Daniel hoisted the fertilizer bag into the bed of his truck. "Good Lord, Daniel!" he said breathlessly as he dropped the fifty-pound bag of phosphorous in the truck bed. "That's a hundred-pound bag, and you picked it up just like it was full of leaves." Billy shook his head and leaned back against the tailgate of the truck.

Daniel smiled but did not speak.

"I need you here at the loading dock." Billy coughed and cleared his throat. "There ain't nothin' here you can't lift."

Daniel's eyes lit up. He had a part-time job cleaning tables at a local pizza place, and on weekends he took up tickets at the movie theater. But there was nothing steady, and he was lucky to have those jobs in such a small town as Hopeful. A stressed economy had just about stopped all hiring.

"You mean it?" he asked enthusiastically.

Billy puckered his lips and rubbed his neck with his bare hand. "Let me talk to Dad about it." He tapped Daniel on the shoulder. "He wants me to work inside at the counter a couple days a week, and to travel out in the counties with seed and fertilizer some, too. I don't know how all that is going to work out, but maybe a morning or two will be open for you. What do you think?"

Daniel smiled. "Tell me when, and I will be here." He had always liked his visits to the store. The Meeks were kind to him. Billy and he were the same age and had attended the same school, although they had only a few classes together. Most of Daniel's classes were in special education. But he had mixed with the other students often. He knew Billy well and liked him.

"I'll let you know something soon," Billy promised as he walked toward the storage room.

Daniel waved goodbye and climbed into his truck. He looked at his wristwatch. It was almost noon. He started the engine and pulled away from the loading area and onto the main street. Three blocks down the street, he pulled over in front of Lucy's Café. He liked Lucy's fresh chicken salad sandwiches and potato wedges. He ate lunch there twice a week.

"Hello, Daniel," Lucy called out as the tall young man entered the café. "I've got one ready for you, and your wedges will be up in a minute." The woman was a bundle of energy.

"Hi, Lucy." Daniel sat down at the front table and looked out the window onto Main Street. A pretty waitress brought him a glass of water, along with a knife and fork rolled up in a napkin. "Thank you, Rita." Daniel smiled as he looked up.

Rita Sedgeway was a petite, young mother-to-be. She was nineteen years old and unmarried. Lucy had given her the waitress job when the girl had shown up at her door with a suitcase in her hand, ten dollars in her pocket, and the promise of an uncertain future written across her pretty forehead. That had been two months ago. It was a good thing for Rita that Lucy Wenby was such a soft-hearted woman. The older woman's past fueled her compassion for Rita. Lucy had been left holding the bills and a baby bottle a time or two in her own life. She knew how hollow a promise could be. And she knew when someone needed her help. Lucy was by no means wealthy, but she did all right. She lived alone, above the café, and her children were grown and lived away. She had given Rita the small, extra bedroom at the back of her apartment. There was no rent, a meager salary, and whatever tips Rita could get.

Rita was happy to have the job. Daniel liked her. She was kind to him and always spent time talking with him.

"What are you doing today, Daniel?" Rita smiled and waited, her hands in the front pocket of her apron.

"I am going to plant sunflowers today." Daniel was comfortable with Rita, and spoke with relative ease.

"Oh, I love sunflowers. Where are you going to plant them?"

"I already planted them in the garden. And now, I'm going to plant them in the fields."

The door to the café opened, and two women came in and sat down. "Gotta work." Rita spoke softly and walked over to the women's table.

Daniel knew most everyone in Hopeful. But he had never seen the two women who took the table near the front door. They were obviously passing through town on their way some place else. He listened to their sophisticated speech as they ordered. Daniel assumed they were mother and daughter.

"I'll have the chicken salad plate and tea with no sugar or lemon," the older woman said politely.

Rita listened without writing down their orders. She had a wonderful memory. Daniel was impressed with her ability to remember several orders at once.

"And I'll have the same," said the younger woman.

Daniel noticed the young woman looking at Rita as her mother was ordering.

"When are you due?" she asked.

"November," Rita answered. "And you?"

The young woman touched her extended belly and smiled. "I'm due in October," she answered. "My husband and I are so excited."

Rita smiled politely. But Daniel knew she was hurt. There was no wedding ring on her finger, and the young woman she waited on could see that. Rita walked back to the kitchen, away from the whispers of the two women. When she returned, she brought Daniel his sandwich and wedges and tea for the two women. There were no more attempts at fake friendliness from the women, and when they left, Lucy did not invite them back. She knew their kind. The world was full of them.

"Don't you have a second thought about those two, honey. They got issues you don't want to know about." Lucy's advice to Rita was quick and free.

Rita was quiet for a minute. She stood beside Lucy and stared out the front window. She waited as the mother and daughter climbed into their over-sized SUV and pulled away. "Well, maybe. But at least that girl has a family."

"So do you, Rita." Lucy looked up from her order book and caught the sad expression on Rita's face. "You've got me and Daniel over there." She looked across the room at the young man who sat quietly eating his lunch.

Daniel heard what Lucy said. He smiled but did not look up.

Rita felt sorry that she had voiced her thought. She knew that Lucy cared for her just like a mother would. And Daniel was like the older brother she never had.

Daniel wiped his mouth with his napkin and stood up. "I'll be back in a minute," he said. Lucy and Rita watched him open the front door.

Rita turned to Lucy. "Where do you think he's going?"

Lucy opened her hands and shrugged her shoulders. She knew Daniel well enough to attempt an answer to Rita's question, but she did not speak.

Several minutes passed, and four customers were seated before Daniel returned and resumed eating his lunch. When he finished eating, he walked to the cash register and left three dollars and fifty cents on the counter. Lucy was turning over a grilled cheese sandwich in the kitchen and could see Daniel at the counter. She pushed through the swinging shutters that were the doors to the kitchen and gave him a hug. "I saw what you brought Rita, you sweetheart."

Daniel smiled. "Bye, Lucy," was all he said.

Rita picked up the dollar tip that Daniel had left beside his plate. But it was the long-stemmed red rose, wrapped in green paper, he had left propped between the salt and pepper shakers that touched her heart. He always knew when she needed him the most.

"Thank you, Daniel." Rita held the rose in her hand and spoke softly as Daniel walked toward her. She put out her arms and stepped into the big embrace of his long, strong arms. "You always know just what I need."

Daniel squeezed the young woman and then opened the front door. "I'll see you at church tomorrow, Rita."

Rita smiled. "I'll be there." She looked back at Lucy as Daniel stepped outside and walked to his truck. Rita held up the rose for Lucy to see. Lucy reached under the counter and placed a long-neck vase next to the cash register. She pointed to it and went back into the kitchen. Rita poured the water from Daniel's glass into the vase and placed the rose in it.

By twelve-fifteen the lunch crowd had filled the café, and Rita kept busy. She forgot about the two women who rode in the SUV. Each time she walked by the rose that Daniel had brought her from the florist two doors down the street, she felt inner peace. She knew she had found a home in Hopeful. The rose was a reminder from Daniel. She knew its meaning. It was his way of telling her that no matter how tough life could be, he was there for her. There were no strings attached to his friendship. That is what made him special to her.

Rita was mopping up milk from a child's over-turned glass when the front door opened and in walked Billy Meeks. The noonday sun fell on his broad shoulders like a golden cape as he stood in the doorway and scanned the room for a table. All the tables were occupied, but there was one stool available at the counter. Billy spotted it and walked over to it. His eyes found Rita's as he sat down, and he grinned.

Rita refilled the child's milk glass. "Hi, Billy," she said with a blink of her long eyelashes.

"Hello, Rita." Billy could not take his eyes off the young woman.

Rita wiped the counter in front of him with a clean, white cloth and set a glass of ice water down. "What'll it be today?"

Billy did not break eye contact as he answered. "The soup and grilled cheese, no pickle."

"You got it." Rita's heart felt as if it were about

to jump out of her chest. *I've got to pull back here*, she thought. *This is no time for another try at a relationship.* Thoughts such as these ran through her mind each time she waited on the handsome young man. She had met Billy through Daniel. It was Daniel who had encouraged her to go out with Billy. They had caught a movie together and dinner.

"He's good." That's what Daniel had told her regarding his childhood friend. She trusted Daniel's judgement of people. There were few in the town of Hopeful Daniel did not know. It was important to have such a friend, especially for a newcomer with no family ties to the area. As far as anyone knew, Rita Sedgeway had stepped off a bus from nowhere, onto the corner of Main and Oak Streets, with little more than the clothes on her back. No one knew that she was the only daughter of John and Eva Sedgeway, an upper middle-class couple from Dayton, Ohio. Few could have imagined the neglect she had felt from her self-centered alcoholic mother, or the fear that haunted her nights due to the presence of an over-attentive and painfully lonely father. How could anyone know Rita Sedgeway? As much as she loved Lucy, she had not told her everything about her life. But Daniel knew it all. She could talk freely with him. He had listened without interjecting his thoughts or opinions. And when he at last knew her story, he kept it to himself. There had been no judgement from him—only the acceptance of her friendship. The secrets of her past were safe with Daniel, and somehow the burden of her self-guilt was lessened through his knowing. She could at least open her mind to the possibility that she could someday trust again. Billy Meeks had no idea how far she had come. And Rita had not yet seen how determined he could be.

Rita placed a glass of ice tea on the counter in front of Billy. "Daniel was here for lunch today," she said.

Billy patted the crushed ice that rose just above the rim of his glass with his forefinger until it was uniformly even. He pressed a clear, plastic straw through the icy slush until it struck the bottom of the glass. He slowly stirred the tea. Rita watched him. She waited for his perfect lips to open. "He came by the store today." Billy chuckled and shook his head. "Dad said he bought us out of sunflower seeds and wanted some more." Billy lowered his head and sucked on the straw. The ice tea felt good in his throat. He swallowed then straightened in his seat. "Said he's gonna plant the old cornfield up there in sunflowers. Can you imagine that?"

"He's already planted the garden area," Rita added. She was not surprised. She knew Daniel too well to be surprised by his seemingly instant passions.

Billy shrugged. "Well, he's gonna need some help if he wants to plant that old cornfield. It hasn't been plowed and disked since Mr. Taylor died. And I know Daniel doesn't even know how to start that old Massey Ferguson tractor. It's been sitting untouched in the Taylor shed for three years."

Rita tapped her fingertips on the countertop before she ventured her thought. "But you know how to start it, don't you Billy?" Her thin, dark eyebrows crept up her forehead as she waited for an answer.

Clever girl, Billy thought. "I know how to drive it, but if the engine needs work, I'm afraid I'm lost." Billy knew where she was going with her inquiry, so he jumped ahead. "Maybe you'd wanna drive up there with me tomorrow after church, and I'll take a look at it." He laid his straw next to his glass and sipped his tea.

Rita heard him crunch ice between his teeth. And then the lips she thought were perfect stretched into a wide grin.

"Well, I, uh, don't know." Rita wanted to say yes, but her reluctance was instinctive. She really liked Billy Meeks, but she was afraid of moving too fast into a relationship. There was so much he did not know about her. Things she was not ready to explain. She watched him rear back and push his long fingers through his auburn hair. The muscles in his shoulders and upper arms bulged underneath his tan T-shirt.

"Come on, Rita," he urged with a smile.

God, you are so good looking, Rita thought. *What am I doing?*

A blue-haired woman sitting at a corner table raised her empty tea glass and caught Rita's attention. She smiled at the woman. "On Sundays, I have lunch up there with Daniel and his grandmother," she said as she gripped the tea pitcher's handle. "We finish eating around one o'clock."

Lucy set a plate with Billy's sandwich and a bowl of soup next to it on the kitchen window counter. Rita brought the order over to Billy. "Maybe I'll see you up there tomorrow afternoon?"

Billy leaned forward, his handsome face engulfed in the fog of steam from his soup. He inhaled the aroma and grinned. "I'll be there."

Rita's heart raced as she turned her attention to the blue-haired lady at the corner table.

Billy watched her walk away. He loved to see her walk.

"Oh, Lord, Miz T." Rosie Holman placed the telephone back in its stand on the kitchen counter and turned to Mary, who stood at the sink, rinsing out her tea cup under the faucet. "April Snead has done killed herself."

"When did it happen?" Mary set the cup down beside the sink and walked to the kitchen table. She pulled out a chair and sat down, her hands palms-down on the table.

Rosie walked over and stood by the dining room window. "Henry says it happened early this mornin'. She was alone in the house. It ain't her day to keep her grandchildren." Rosie lifted her face and rubbed her thick neck with an ever-present handkerchief she usually carried tucked in her cleavage. "He said she'd lost her job over at the store where she worked. Had some health problems, too."

Mary looked over at Rosie. "How did Henry hear about it?"

"Our oldest…." Rosie started.

"Oden." Mary knew the son of Rosie and Henry Holman. He was a sheriff's deputy.

"Yes ma'am." Rosie nodded. "He just got back from April's house. Said it's mighty sad and grim over there."

Mary rubbed the age spots on the back of her hand. She knew April Snead as a good, hard-working woman. April had lived a difficult life. But she had done her best, raising her children and giving them everything she could. And she loved her grandchildren. But there was never enough money. Most folks would say she was poor, always working for meager wages. The clerk's job at the corner store was the most steady employment she had probably ever had. But business was off everywhere. The recession had lasted longer than anyone had expected. Everyone was affected. Employers were cutting back in every way they could. Otherwise, they would be forced to close their doors.

"I don't see how somebody can take their own life like that, Miz T. But you hearin' about it every day now. Soldiers are doin' it overseas and here at home. What is it that people are doin' such a thing these days?" Rosie touched her lips with her fingers. She looked at Mary and waited.

The older woman took a deep breath before she answered. "You see it every night on the television news, Rosie. You hear it on the radio and read it in the newspaper. The preacher is going to talk about it in church tomorrow. He'll mention words like greed, mistrust, and faithlessness. He'll talk about a change. Everybody is talking about change. But there's not going to be a change, Rose. Change is just a word. In a time of unrest, words like that sprout up to calm those who are fearful and stall those who are dangerous. Words can be comforting, but also deceiving. It's a 'wait-and-see' time in our lives. But not everyone can wait." Mary stood up slowly and walked over to the window where she stood beside Rosie and looked out into the flower garden. She folded her arms and continued. "Folks need faith, Rosie. And I don't just mean faith in your fellow man. I mean faith in God. That is what gives words like 'change' meaning and power. But it has to come from within. So many people have lost that faith. They misplaced it, or somehow saw it reborn in politics and government programs." Mary shrugged. "Progress. That's another great word. But it has no power without God's faith behind it." There was silence between the two women before Mary continued. "April was tired. The harshness of the world tore at the foundation of her faith, until she found herself in a hole so dark she could not see the light. She lost hope. And in a dreadful moment, she reached for an end to it all. The world we have made is what is happening to people, Rosie. Our souls are being consumed by it." Mary turned and walked back into the kitchen. She filled a pitcher with water from the faucet and began watering colorful flowers in small containers on the windowsill above the sink.

"What are you gonna tell Daniel 'bout April, Miz T?" The two women listened as Daniel's truck came into the driveway. "How in the world are you gonna tell that young man 'bout his friend?" Rosie's voice was so sad.

Mary put the water pitcher on the counter, then turned and faced Rosie. "He might already know."

Daniel would not speak of what had happened to his friend. Perhaps he did not understand it all. Who could? But for nights after he learned the sad news of April Snead's suicide, Mary could hear his heart-wrenching sobs. His pain she could not console with her words. So she let him cry it out. He did not leave his room for three days and when finally he came out, Mary found him in the flower garden, sitting on the swing. That May morning, she finished watering her flowers before she went and sat down next to him.

"I'm glad to see you outside, Daniel." Mary laid her frail hand over his as she spoke. "Rita called last night to ask about you. She has been worried, since you wouldn't come out when she and Billy were here on Sunday."

Daniel did not speak. Mary knew he would not be able to express his thoughts concerning April Snead with words. But the gesture of his hand touching hers meant that he was coming back to her. "April was just tired, Daniel. She must have been so tired."

Daniel remained silent but nodded his head.

Mary decided to change the subject. "While you were inside, Billy looked at your grandfather's tractor. He said it needs some work, and he's sending a man up here this afternoon to fix it." Mary studied the profile of Daniel's face. He looked so much like his father. She swallowed her sadness.

"Rita and Billy said they would help you plant the cornfield."

Daniel swallowed and looked up, searching for the words he wanted to say. "My sunflowers out in the garden will be coming up soon, Mimi."

Mary leaned against the arm of the young man. "I know they will."

"They are going to be beautiful, like my dream."

Mary squeezed Daniel's arm with her hand. "It'll be just like the sun has come down into the garden."

Daniel smiled. "My dream," he said softly.

"Your dream." Mary's words were reassuring. "I know something about sunflowers that might surprise you."

"What?" Daniel asked. He looked at his grandmother.

Mary turned her head to the side and then looked behind her as if she were guarding a desirable secret. "Well, my mother once told me when I was a young girl that if you sleep with a sunflower under your pillow, it will allow you to know the truth of any matter."

"Really?" Daniel was very interested in what his grandmother said. He turned toward her. "Is that really true, Mimi?"

"Maybe you'll find out if it is," Mary responded. "You are sure going to have enough sunflowers to give it a try."

Daniel smiled.

Mary loved his smile.

Isaac Heartwell had the Massey Ferguson tractor running as smoothly as a new one within an hour of his arrival. "Your granddaddy took real good care of this tractor, Daniel," Isaac shouted over the sputtering of the engine. He pulled on the throttle and turned his head to the side, listening. "Yeah, sounds good." He turned the engine off and walked over to where Daniel stood beside a row of plumb trees. "All it needed was a little cleaning, a battery re-charge, and some fuel."

"Can you drive it, Isaac?" Daniel liked the man with the white hair the minute he had met him. He liked Isaac's cheerful attitude and his voice. The voice reminded him of his grandfather.

Isaac scratched the top of his head and half-turned toward the tractor. "Drive it?" he laughed. "I can work that old thing there like she was meant to be worked." He turned back to Daniel. "What ya got in mind?"

Daniel pointed beyond the garden area to the field. "I want to grow sunflowers out there. But it needs to be plowed and..." the young man struggled for the word he wanted.

Isaac caught on fast. "I can plow and disc that field there in one afternoon," he offered.

"You mean it?" Daniel could not believe his luck.

"I'll tell you what, Daniel." He patted Daniel on the shoulder with his thick hand. "You take that five-gallon tank into Hopeful and bring back some diesel fuel, and we'll turn up that field today. You can be dropping seeds on it by tomorrow, if you want to."

"But you have to go back to work." Daniel remembered that Billy Meeks had sent Isaac up the hill. The short, stout man shook his head. "I don't work for Billy."

"Where do you work?" Daniel seemed confused.

"Oh, I move around mostly. Doing a job here and there. Billy's truck broke down there at the bottom of the hill yesterday." Isaac pointed toward town. "I was walking along and saw that he needed some help. That's when he asked me if I knew something about tractors, and I said I did. So he sent me up here, and now we're fixing to get that field ready for sunflowers."

"But I can't pay you much money." Daniel was honest but feared he might lose the one person who could help him with his project. "I've got an apartment up over the garage you can stay in, if you need a place for a while."

Isaac rubbed his chin and looked out at the barn-shaped garage. He looked back at Daniel. "What'll your grandmother say about that?"

Daniel did not hesitate in his response. "I think she will be okay with that, if you help me with my sunflowers."

Isaac clapped his hands together. "All right then, you check with her, and I'll get some air in those tractor tires and grease her joints. Then we'll hook her up to that plow and head for the field." Isaac started for the tractor. "Throw in a meal or two a day with that offer, Daniel, and forget the money. I'll work for food and board."

Daniel waved his hand at the man, but he did not speak. He was halfway to the house.

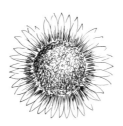

"Isaac is a good man, Mimi. Billy Meeks sent him up to help with the tractor." There was excitement in Daniel's voice as his grandmother sat at the kitchen table and listened. She had seen the old man walking up the driveway earlier and wondered who he was.

"I saw that man comin' round the bend in the road and wondered if maybe he was looking for a handout or somethin!" Rosie said as she entered the kitchen with a stack of folded dish towels in her hands. She placed them down on the kitchen counter and sorted them by color. Then she opened a drawer and stacked the red checked ones on one side and the green checked ones on the other. She closed the drawer and turned around. "But then I figured he won't bad, because the butterflies found him sweet enough to follow him up here. They was all around him."

"He said he would plow the field and disc it for me, Mimi." Daniel looked over at Rosie for encouragement. She winked at him and smiled.

"He's already got the tractor running, and all he needs is some diesel fuel." Daniel waited. He watched his grandmother sip her coffee and place her cup down on the table. He heard the mantle clock in the den begin to chime.

When the chiming ceased, his grandmother spoke. "What does he want for his trouble, Daniel?" She looked at Daniel and then over at Rosie. "These days, people don't just drop by to do good things for others." Mary did not like to be so blunt, but at times it was necessary for effect. To a degree, Daniel was a child in a man's body, torn and often confused by human nature. His reactions to people were instinctive. He did not always recognize the deceitfulness in those he came into contact with. Daniel's heart carried the scars of his mistakes. His soul the bruises. But there was still a light of innocence in him. A beautiful gift, wrapped in a tattered package. And it was his gift to all who were open to it.

Mary Taylor was protective of her grandson. That was her nature. It was the one thing she could be for Daniel as long as it was possible. Her greatest fear was what would become of him when she was no longer there. That fear haunted her.

Rosie was aware of the reasons that caused Mary's hesitation concerning Isaac Heartwell. But she also trusted her own instincts. "Miz T, don't you think it best to speak with Mister Heartwell while Daniel runs into town to get that fuel?" She paused while Mary considered her question.

Daniel could sense that Rosie was on his side, and he took advantage of the moment. "He doesn't want money. He could stay in the apartment until we've finished with the field. And maybe Rosie could fix him something to eat." He looked at Rosie for approval.

"I'd be willin' to do that." Rosie smiled. She opened a cabinet door and retrieved a tea pitcher.

Mary pushed her coffee cup away from her. She stood up and walked to the open window. The sound of the tractor's engine prodded her memory. It had been over three years since she had heard that sound. *Maybe Daniel is right*, she thought. *Maybe Isaac Heartwell is a good man.* "You go on down to the corner store and get the diesel fuel, Daniel," she finally said. "I'll go out and talk with Mr. Heartwell in a few minutes."

Daniel rose from his chair and walked over to his grandmother. He put his long arms around her and pulled her close to him. "He's a good man, Mimi. You'll like him."

Mary looked up and saw the sincerity on Daniel's

face. She touched his cheek with her hand. "Get some cash from my desk drawer before you go. Diesel fuel is expensive these days."

Daniel kissed his grandmother on the forehead and cut his eyes over at Rosie as he left the room.

Mary brought her coffee cup over to the kitchen sink, where she emptied it and rinsed it out. "Maybe in between your winking and meddling, you can fix a glass of tea for me to take out to Mr. Heartwell."

Rosie smiled as she filled the tea kettle with water and set it on the stove burner. "Oh, you know I'll be glad to do it Miz T." The woman hummed a little tune as she moved about. "There's nothin' like a friendly conversation over a glass of sweet iced tea."

"We'll see." Mary made her comment while turning up the volume on the radio at the end of the counter. The two women listened to a story about a man who had been arrested in Australia and charged with setting one of the wildfires that killed more than 180 people there. He was being held in protective custody, to keep him from being mobbed.

Neither woman commented as Mary shook her head, turned and left the room.

Hilda Yeatts looked at the amount on the monitor screen next to her cash register. "That will be $27.95, Daniel." She waited patiently as the tall young man placed a twenty and a ten down on the counter. "Out of thirty," she said as she opened the register. "There you go, sweetie."

Hilda's voice had always sounded happy to Daniel. He knew her and her husband, Tom, well and was fond of them. "Thank you, Hilda." Daniel put his change away.

"What in the world are you buying diesel fuel for?" Hilda was curious and knew Daniel would not mind her question.

"It's for Papa's tractor."

Hilda was surprised. She could not imagine Daniel operating a tractor. "My goodness, Daniel. I know that you work at the pizza place and the theater, but I never took you for a farmer."

Daniel reached into his back pocket and brought out an envelope. "I'm not," he said as he handed the envelope to Hilda. "Do you still teach Sunday School?" he asked.

Hilda took the envelope. "Yes," she answered, while looking at the address on the front. It was directed to the Sunday School classes and written in Daniel's awkward handwriting.

"Can you read this to your Sunday School class?" Daniel asked while arranging several additional envelopes he had pulled out of his pocket.

Hilda opened the unsealed envelope and read the handwritten note inside. When she finished, she smiled. "Of course I'll read it," she said. "Good luck!"

Daniel smiled and turned to leave. "Thank you, Hilda."

Hilda watched him leave. And when her husband came in through the back door a minute later, she handed him Daniel's note.

He read the note and put it back in its envelope. "Well, I'll be. I heard Forrest Meeks saying Daniel had bought fifty pounds of sunflower seeds from the store." Tom scratched his head. "Truth is we were both wondering what he is up to."

"Oh?" Hilda placed the envelope in her pocketbook.

"Yeah. He told Forrest he's going to plant the fields around the place up there with sunflowers."

"But why sunflowers?" Hilda could not imagine the reason.

"Don't know. Forrest says he didn't say why. Just that he'd dreamed it."

"Well, that's going to be a chore. But it explains the diesel fuel."

"Diesel fuel?"

"Yes. He bought it for Frank's tractor."

Tom shrugged his shoulders. "I didn't even know the boy knew anything about operating a tractor."

Hilda put her bag under the counter. "Well, he obviously knows how to inspire people."

Tom thought about Daniel's note. "That he does. You think Mary is behind this?"

A customer walked in the front door, and Hilda

answered her husband quietly. "I don't know, Tom, but that is a beautiful note isn't it?"

By the time Daniel had finished delivering all of the envelopes in his possession, it was after noon. He looked at his wristwatch. *One more stop*, he thought. *I have time for one more stop.*

Benny Lester was sitting in his den watching a special news report when he heard a knock on his front door. The man got up from his chair and walked to the door while the TV anchorman read a news bulletin about a commuter plane that had just crashed into a house near Buffalo, New York. All passengers aboard were feared dead, along with the occupant of the house. Benny tried to clear his head as he opened the front door.

"Hello, Daniel." The short, stout man smiled and extended his hand.

Daniel met his offering with a firm grip. "Hi, Benny."

"Come in." Benny pulled the door open wide and stepped to the side.

Daniel did not move forward. Instead, he opened his mouth and searched the air above his head for the word he needed to begin his sentence. Benny waited.

He knew Daniel well and was very aware of the young man's speech delay. "I won't be able to come to Special Olympics basketball practice today." Daniel spoke slowly and precisely. "But I want you to read this letter to everybody." Daniel handed an envelope to Benny. He positioned his lips and bent his head forward as he labored to finish his thought. "Will you?" he asked.

Benny opened the unsealed envelope and read the note while Daniel waited.

When he finished the letter, Benny smiled and pushed it back into the envelope. He looked into Daniel's eyes. They seemed like dark wells to Benny. Kind, wise, and determined. The older man had always felt there was something about Daniel that separated him from other people. It was in the complexity of his nature. Benny had witnessed Daniel's positive effect on scores of people, young and old. Benny taught Special Education at the Hopeful Elementary School, where Daniel had attended. He knew that Daniel was driven, or guided, by something within him that lifted him beyond the confines of his mental and physical challenges. Benny had once told Mary and Frank Taylor that Daniel's true intelligence could never be determined by standard tests. There were too many variables. Variables that had always made the case of Daniel Taylor intriguing, at the least. Benny had read the comments from the doctors at the Kluge Institute and the Children's Hospital. He knew how they had studied the boy. He read the comments of their amazement, the reports that praised Daniel's determination to reach out and communicate with

66

the world around him. He had devised his own form of sign language before he could utter his first word. That alone was beyond a number that any IQ test could suggest. Daniel possessed an internal strength that would not allow him to go unnoticed.

Benny Lester did not know what it was in Daniel that gave him the ability to touch people. But he knew without a doubt that Daniel had it. It was a beautiful gift, and one far beyond the imaginations of anyone who knew him.

"I'll read it aloud this afternoon, Daniel," Benny promised while tucking the envelope into his shirt pocket. He stepped forward and patted Daniel on the shoulder. "Why sunflowers?"

Daniel smiled but did not answer. Perhaps he could not. "Thank you, Benny," was all he said.

Benny watched his former student walk away. Then he closed the door and walked back into his den, where the CNN anchorman was speaking over a film clip of massive ice cliffs breaking off and sliding into the frigid ocean. "New satellite and other data on the melting of Antarctic glaciers are causing concern among scientists who say it's happening faster than anticipated over a wide area." The anchor went on to say, "The result could eventually be an unprecedented rise in sea levels."

Benny picked up the remote control and turned the volume on the television down as a segment began about African children who were dying of AIDS.

"Who was at the door, Benny?" Benny's wife, Lynn, called from the kitchen, where the sound from the CNN report spilled from the small set on the counter and bled between her words.

Benny heard the question, but he did not answer. His mind was lost in thought. When Lynn walked into the den, she found her husband sitting in his chair with an open letter in his hand and a whisper on his lips she could hardly make out. "What, Benny?" she asked.

Benny looked up at his wife and repeated the word he had whispered. "Sunflowers."

Isaac Heartwell locked the last pin on the plow as Mary Taylor approached him. "There now," he said as he raised up and took off his straw hat. He bent slightly forward at his waist. "You must be Daniel's grandmother."

"Hello, Mr. Heartwell." Mary offered the man a glass of iced tea as she greeted him.

"Thank you, Mrs. Taylor." Isaac took the glass and sipped the cold sweetness on its rim. "Umm, that's fine tea, ma'am," he said. "I don't recollect any better for quite a spell." He enjoyed a long drink and placed the half-full glass on the tractor's back fender.

Mary saw that the man had finished attaching the

plow to her husband's tractor. A used grease gun was lying on the ground close to a tractor tire.

Isaac followed her gaze and reached down and picked up the grease gun. "Hadn't been greased for a long time."

Mary smiled sparingly. "That's a mighty big field out there, Mr. Heartwell," she said while looking past the man. Her blue eyes came back to his. "Has Daniel asked you to plow it for him?"

Isaac put his hat back on his head and looked around at the rolling hills. The old corn field did not seem so big to him. "It's just right, I reckon, for what that young fella has in mind, ma'am."

Mary pondered the man's response. "Well, Mr. Heartwell, I'm really not sure what he has in mind. Are you?"

Isaac understood Mary's cautious nature and her careful questions. "Said he dreamed it up, ma'am. Wants to bring the sun down into the field."

"The sun?" Mary recalled saying those same words to her grandson. She wondered now how he had interpreted them.

Isaac locked a lynch pin onto a stable bar and continued. "Your grandson is a special young man." The man was a master at clever avoidance. "I guess when he dreams up something and sets his mind to making it happen, it becomes a reality to him." Isaac opened the toolbox beside the tractor seat and placed a screwdriver inside it. He closed the lid and looked at the attractive woman questioning him. "You know him best, ma'am. I reckon you'll figure it out."

Mary Taylor studied Isaac's face as she listened to him. He was straight on. There was no glancing away when he spoke. She sensed that he was genuine. There was nothing in his demeanor that warned her to be overly cautious. But she could not hide her nature. "Where are you from, Mr. Heartwell?" she asked, knowing he would expect such a question.

"Everywhere." The man smiled as he answered. He noticed an eyebrow creeping up the woman's forehead. "That is, I've lived in a lot of places," he added quickly.

"But where's home?"

Isaac thumped the brim of his hat with his finger. "Wherever I lay my hat, ma'am, is home enough for me." The man's answer was certainly evasive but delivered with a good measure of gaiety.

Mary thought that perhaps he was the kind of person who would make the best of any situation, even homelessness. So many people had lost their jobs and homes in recent years that she was not surprised that one of them would find his way to her door through Daniel. After all, Daniel had always had a knack for gathering stray people.

Rita Sedgeway was a perfect example. A young and pregnant girl, jilted by her less-than-responsible boyfriend and cut off by her self-absorbed parents. It was Daniel who had noticed her alone and crying on a bench at the bus stop in town. He had given the girl money for food and taken her to Lucy Wenby, who had given her a job and a place to stay above the café. Rita had told Mary that she was scared and alone before the day Daniel came into her life. She had said he was like an angel to her. Mary understood that. She had heard it before. It was not that Daniel actually tried to be caring of others. Some people are just born that way. Daniel could be fooled at times by deceitful people, but for the most part, he was a good judge of character. Mary had come to love Rita, and there were many others over the years that her grandson had befriended, most of whom were in need of a friend such as he.

Isaac Heartwell was the latest. An old man down on his luck and homeless, but with a good and willing nature. Isaac's personality was right up Daniel's alley. And the man seemed to know tractors, too.

"Well, Mr. Heartwell," Mary began as Daniel drove his truck up the long driveway. "You are welcome to stay in the apartment there." She pointed toward the garage. "The bed clothes are fresh, and the shower has good pressure."

Daniel stopped his truck in the driveway on the other side of the rose fence.

"Supper is at six-thirty, unless you are out in the field at that time." Mary watched her grandson get out of the truck and walk around to the truck's tailgate, where he opened it and pulled a red fuel container toward him. "Daniel can bring it to you out there, if need be."

Isaac nodded his head. "I appreciate that, Mrs. Taylor. And I'm glad to help your young man."

Daniel walked over and set the fuel can next to the tractor. He reached into his pants pocket and brought out the change Hilda Yeatts had given him and handed it to his grandmother.

"You might want to open up those windows in the apartment and let it air out a bit, Daniel. We don't want Mr. Heartwell to find it stuffy up there." Mary nodded her head toward Isaac as she spoke and then turned and walked away.

Daniel smiled. He knew his grandmother would like Isaac. How could she not?

Isaac was right when he said he would have the old cornfield ready for Daniel's sunflower seeds when night fell over the rolling hills that surrounded the town of Hopeful. Daniel opened a bag of mammoth sunflower seeds and sifted through them with his fingers. "You think one bag will be enough, Isaac?" Daniel could not realize how many seeds were in a fifty-pound sack.

Isaac chuckled as he came down off the tractor and peered into the seed sack Daniel had brought back from Meeks Farm and Seed Store. "You've got plenty of seeds for that field, Daniel." Isaac reached down and gathered a few seeds between his fingers.

"How do you want to plant them?" He let the seeds fall into the bag.

Daniel pulled the top of the sack together and tied it with a length of twine he had gotten from the tractor shed. "Three feet apart, with four feet of space between the rows."

"Is that what you did out there in the garden?"

Daniel nodded his head.

"Good, then." Isaac took off his straw hat and rubbed his fingers through his hair. "We'll get on that in the morning."

"Billy is coming up to help." Daniel stood up and lifted the seed bag into the truck bed. He closed the truck's gate and turned to Isaac. "Rita is coming, too." He paused as if he were thinking. "And some others."

Isaac put his hat back on. "Well, Daniel, the more the better. You've got a lot of seeds there, and you seem intent on dropping them by hand. That's going to take a while."

Daniel looked at Isaac. There was a seriousness in his voice when he spoke. "They have to be planted by hand."

Isaac seemed to understand. He patted Daniel on the shoulder. "I'll bet that was in the dream, wasn't it?"

Daniel looked toward the field but did not reply. There was something else he wanted to tell Isaac. It was about the hands needed to plant the seeds that would bring the sun into the field. But he did not tell what he knew. And Isaac did not ask.

Daniel was tired when he walked into the movie theater later that night. His work schedule was from eight until midnight. He greeted his co-workers with his usual smile. He swept the floors and made his clean-up rounds after the movies were over. And, in between, he tore and stacked tickets.

At twelve-fifteen, Daniel walked out of the theater and made his way to his truck. The parking lot was still almost full of vehicles. Daniel heard the sound of wicked laughter before a tall, shabbily-dressed young man stepped in front of him. Daniel tried to walk around the man he recognized from Forrest Meek's store days earlier, but the man would not let him pass.

"Hey, hold on a minute." The man slurred his words as he pushed at Daniel's chest with his out-stretched hand.

"What have we got here?" Another voice came from behind. Daniel turned his head and recognized another face from that same day in the store. He immediately remembered what Forrest had said about the two Scaggs brothers. A feeling of dread came over him as he tried again to step around the man blocking his way. But again, he felt the thud of the man's hand on his chest. Daniel stood still and quiet.

"Hey, Bucky." The man standing in his way tilted his head to one side and peeked around Daniel at his brother. "I remember this dude." He staggered back one step, then came in close. Daniel could smell the liquor on his breath.

"Who is he, Lonnie?" the man behind Daniel asked while walking around him.

The one called Lonnie studied Daniel's face for a minute with bulging, bloodshot eyes. "This is that idiot that almost knocked me down in the feed store last week." He poked his forefinger into Daniel's chest. "You remember me, don't you, Idiot?"

"Leave him alone, Lonnie," a girl called out of the darkness from where the two men had appeared.

Daniel looked over and saw Del Jenkins scoot out of the back seat of a mud-spattered Bronco. She fastened the top button of her blouse as she slammed the door of the vehicle and walked out of the shadows.

"Shut up, Del." Bucky spat on the pavement in front of the girl. "This ain't none of your business."

The girl straightened her short skirt and flung her long, black hair back over her narrow shoulders. She stood her ground with her hands on her hips. "His name is Daniel Taylor, and he's a friend of mine from school."

"Well, do tell, Del," Lonnie spoke with a smirk. "Me and Bucky thought you liked your men, well, normal, like us!" He looked at his brother and laughed.

Bucky Scaggs emitted a raspy chuckle. He shoved Daniel and smirked when the tall, quiet man stumbled to regain his balance.

"Yeah, Del." There was menace in Bucky's voice. "This one can't hardly stand up. Look at him."

The two brothers snickered.

Del had not seen Daniel since they had graduated from high school. But she would not have forgotten him. He had been kind to her when other kids in school were not. She knew him as a gentle and caring person, quiet, and attentive to others. His main courses had been in special education, but they had shared a food services class for two years and had helped to cater several school functions in their junior and senior years. Daniel once told her she was pretty. It was a compliment she had never forgotten, for there was no motive behind it. Only the sincerity he was known for.

Lonnie and Bucky Scaggs did not know Daniel Taylor. They had come to town only recently, after inheriting John Scaggs' house and property. John was a small-time farmer. Retired and ill, he had no family to leave his estate to other than the sons of his only brother. But Lonnie and Bucky were not farmers. They were off-and-on mechanics, who worked only enough to support their less-than-admirable lifestyles. As long as they had enough money for the liquor, drugs, and women they desired, they believed they were satisfied. But that form of satisfaction does not feed the soul. Nor does it build character or self-esteem. And in those areas, the Scaggs brothers were sorely lacking. Had they understood their misgivings, they might have had an idea why they were bored most of the time and hollow inside. But the truth was, they were just not that bright.

That night in the movie theater parking lot, Daniel had become their lark. He had walked into their incidental trap like a hundred people before him. And when he recognized the situation he was in, he withdrew into the only defensive mode he had ever known. Defiant silence.

After he regained his balance from Bucky's sudden shove, he walked back to his place and stood with straight shoulders. His dark eyes glared into the criminous gazes of his nemeses. He did not blink.

Daniel's physical strength was more than a match for the two scrappy troublemakers. But his lack of physical coordination would have rendered him helpless in a fight with them. They did not know that. They only saw that he was not backing down from them. The cowards they were began to creep through the facade of superiority the liquor had afforded them. A tense minute of silence was interrupted by moviegoers spilling out into the parking lot as their movies ended.

Del stepped between the brothers and Daniel. "Leave him alone, Lonnie," she said in disgust. "Those people won't stand by and let the two of you harm him, and neither will I."

Lonnie looked at Del and then over at his brother. He sensed a nervousness in Bucky's eyes. He looked back at Daniel. "This is a cruddy dump of a town." He shoved Del out of his way and pressed his finger into Daniel's chest as he uttered his last four words. "We'll see you again." Lonnie then looked over at Del as if he was sizing her up with his eyes. "You shut up and get back in the Bronco." He tapped his brother on the arm and walked toward the vehicle. "C'mon, Bucky. This ain't worth our time."

Del stood beside Daniel. She looked up at him with tears in her eyes. "I'm sorry," she said, ashamed.

"I'll take you home, Del." Daniel did not want the young woman to get into the Bronco. He sensed she could be harmed. "Let me take you home." His words came slow. There was kindness in his eyes as he looked down at her.

"C'mon Del!" Bucky shouted as his brother revved the Bronco's engine.

She looked over at the brothers and then back at Daniel.

Lonnie jerked the Bronco into gear and pulled up beside her. "Are you comin' or not?"

"Not." Del did not even look at Lonnie as she answered. And she ignored the expletive he spat at her as he pulled away.

"I'd appreciate the ride home, Daniel." Del leaned into her friend and clung to his arm.

Daniel walked her to his truck in silence.

Mary Taylor walked along the slate walkway her husband had laid years before as a winding pathway through her flower garden. The garden used to be the yard and was sometimes still referred to as that, even though the grass was now relegated to small terraces. Shrubs and flowers had long ago taken preference over the bluegrass and fescue that Frank had tended to so carefully. He had not minded, though, especially in his later years, as his health began to decline. It was better to surround oneself with color and fragrance when the world, according to his wife, had become so black and white.

Frank had laid out the garden with Mary's input. He drew it on paper, and added to it often. A stone border, a grassy terrace, a split-rail fence, bordered by roses and wisteria. There were peach, plum, and apple trees growing on the edges of the garden. A pear tree stood at slanted attention at the corner of the concrete patio. The slate and gravel walkways were laid so that his wife could water all of her plants and flowers with ease. Water spigots were installed at various intervals, where short hoses could be fastened and kept for convenience.

Mary loved her garden. It was a little paradise she and her husband had made together. A shared love for flowers and plants that had kept them close. The narrow walkways were like memory lanes to her. Even now, she could often imagine Frank watering the flowers or trimming the shrubs. She could close her eyes and hear his voice on a windy morning when the dew sparkled like diamonds in the sunlight on the leaves. The arbor he had built for his grape vines had filled in during the years since his death, and Mary sometimes sat on the bench in that shaded corridor, where they used to talk and plan. Life, as love, was a beautiful but fleeting gift. Mary thought of it that way. She had come to believe that a lifetime was like a single breath of air to God. And love was the ultimate reason for one's being. She wondered if the people of the world had forgotten that or, had they really ever known it.

"How was the chicken salad, Mr. Heartwell?" Mary quietly approached Isaac. She was glad to see she had not startled the man who was sitting alone at the patio table.

"It was delicious, Mrs. Taylor, thank you." Isaac pushed the empty plate away from him, scooted his chair back, and rose to his feet. "Please join me," he offered, touching the back of another chair.

Mary took the chair he offered and sat down.

Isaac continued. "You must tell Rosie how I enjoyed my supper this evening."

"I will," Mary responded as she looked at the man she had only recently met. She thought he was rather odd, though not in a bad way. He was a short, stout man who looked to be in his mid-sixties. His hair was fine and white. There were no wrinkles on his face to record his years, and his eyes were bright blue and alive. His body moved with the agility of a younger man. She saw an outward strength about him, but sensed inner wisdom.

"Daniel will be happy to see your progress on the field."

"Oh, yes." Isaac placed his hands down on the table. "The soil is rich around your place. I'm sure his sunflowers will do just fine."

Mary shook her head and smiled. "Sunflowers," she said as she looked up at the darkening sky.

"You still wonder why, don't you, Mrs. Taylor?" Isaac leaned back in his chair and rested his arms on the chair's wide armrests.

"Mary." Mary wanted an informal chat. "Please."

Isaac bowed his head slightly toward the woman. He knew instinctively she wanted to talk with him. He was not surprised. "Well, Mary, what do you think is in the mind of your grandson?" Almost as an afterthought, he added, "And I am Isaac to you."

Mary folded her arms and said, "I'm not sure, Isaac. I guess I know Daniel's heart better than I know his mind."

"I'm sure he was a joy to you and your late husband."

"Oh, yes. After his father's death, it seemed as though the world was revolving without Frank and me. The days were long. The nights seemed endless." Mary swallowed and cleared her voice. "And then one morning, Frank called me out to the dogwood tree by the cedar swing." She pointed with one finger. "And when I got there, he was holding that beautiful baby boy in his arms. A letter explained the mother's fear of raising him and why she couldn't." Mary pressed her lips together. She looked up at the faint stars that had begun emerging in the night sky. Then she continued. "We never knew her name. Stephen, our son, had not told us of her. He never even knew he had a son."

"So, you named him Daniel?"

"No. Actually, his mother gave him that name. In the letter, she wrote that he was named for the Daniel in the Old Testament of the Bible. The one whose faith saved him in the den of lions."

"Interesting." Isaac liked Mary. He sensed a depth to her as she spoke.

"Yes, it is. And Frank and I wondered if she knew that Daniel was Stephen's middle name."

"Oh, the mysteries of life, Mary."

Mary smiled and agreed. "Daniel was a miracle to us," she confided. "A bright star out of a blackened night."

"I'm sure there have been challenges." Isaac made no attempt to avoid the truth of Daniel's condition.

"We met them as they came and still do. But his lust for life and love of people has always driven Daniel over most of the obstacles in his path."

"I was impressed with him the moment I met him. He finds a way to get his point across."

Mary laughed. "Yes, he does."

"What frightens you most, Mary?"

Mary chose her words thoughtfully. "What frightens me for him is what I can only imagine."

Isaac waited for her to continue.

"I have a great fear of what this world will do to him when I'm gone."

"This world?" Isaac knew what Mary was getting at. But he needed to hear her say it. "What is it about this world, Mary?"

Mary looked down at her side and touched the young, pale petal of a spring flower that grew at the edge of the patio. She inhaled at length, then exhaled slowly. "The world," she repeated. She paused for several moments before she continued. "I think that God has lost His patience with the people of the world. He gave us a place of such color and beauty. Paradise. And through some strange desire to prove ourselves great and powerful, we have practically ruined it. The air and the water and the soil are poisoned. Our cement creations have covered the garden we were supposed to tend. Man's choices to better himself have led to his spiritual desperation. I feel the world has lost its color, Isaac. Man's spirit is unfulfilled. His hopes for a better world are clouded by greed and failure. Sadness has turned to anger. It is now a dangerous world, even beyond anything we have seen before. And that is what frightens me, not only for Daniel, but for his generation and the next."

"But there are still good people in the world, Mary." Isaac heard the fear in Mary's words, but he sensed a hopefulness in her character. "Do you agree?"

A faint breeze crept through the garden. Chilled, Mary unrolled her shirt sleeves and buttoned them around her thin wrists. She studied Isaac's face for long moments before she answered his question. "Yes. I think there are good people left in the world. But they have become quiet. They whisper, while others shout. They perform their good deeds in silence and seem to be waiting for something."

"Waiting for what?"

Mary responded thoughtfully. "For their hopes, prayers, and dreams to come true."

Isaac appreciated Mary's concern. He understood her in ways she could not have known. For Isaac Heartwell was much more than the good-natured rolling stone he seemed. And his presence in Hopeful was not by chance.

"I have hope now," Mary offered.

"And why is that?"

Mary found it easy to talk to Isaac, as if he were an old and trusted friend. Her earlier suspicion of him had disappeared during their first conversation. Mary swallowed hard and dabbed at a tear in the corner of her eye with her finger. "I hope. I even find myself praying that Daniel will see his dream come true."

"That's good, Mary." Isaac's smile reflected his compassion for the woman. "With you in his corner, how can that young man go wrong?"

Mary's little laugh felt good. She suddenly felt her spirits lift. "All he wants is to plant a field of sunflowers," she said. "Sunflowers." She shook her head.

Isaac just smiled. The best part of his job was knowing.

It was early Sunday afternoon when Mary Taylor walked to the cedar swing and strained her eyes to see across the garden to the hillside where her husband used to grow corn. Crows cawed in the distance, while a ruby-throated hummingbird swooped down from a high perch and hovered next to a feeder she had filled with nectar the day before. The voices of excited children echoed from the driveway that circled Mary's home and garden.

The sky was cloudless when Billy and Rita drove up the driveway. Billy opened his truck door. "Mornin', Miz Taylor," he called while turning to gather boxes that had been stacked on the seat between him and Rita.

Rita slid out of the truck on the passenger's side. "Hello, Mary." She walked toward the older woman.

Mary saw the stacked, flat boxes in Rita's arms. "Let me help you with those." She reached out and lifted two boxes from Rita's armload. "My goodness! What in the world have you brought with you?"

Billy joined the two women. Mary chuckled when she could see only his eyes above the boxes he carried.

"You're carrying a lazy-man's load, Billy," she teased. "Don't drop it." She led the couple to the kitchen door and called for Rosie.

The big woman appeared in an instant and pushed open the screen door. She took the boxes from Mary and walked to the dining-room table, where she set the boxes down among numerous other containers. The house smelled like a church banquet. "Lord have mercy, Miz T," she exclaimed as she made room on the table. "I ain't seen the likes of this since our reunion at the church last year."

"Lucy sent over all these ham biscuits." Rita lowered her stack of boxes down on the kitchen counter. "There must be three hundred or more."

"We've got chicken wings, too." Billy stood at the dining-room table and waited as Rosie unloaded his arms. "There are some cakes and pies still in the truck." He touched Rita's forearm with his fingers as he walked by her. "I'll bring them in."

Rita smiled and watched him walk out the kitchen door. She blushed when she noticed Mary smiling at her.

"He's a good one, Rita." Mary saw the spark between the two young people. She was not surprised at seeing them together more and more. Daniel had told her that Rita and Billy were meant for each other. The only person requiring convincing was Rita. Mary knew that Daniel had done his part in bringing them together. Nature would take care of the rest. That, and time.

Rita joined her hands and smiled. "I couldn't

believe all the cars along the driveway. And the children!" She walked over to the door that led out to the patio. "They all came, Mary."

"He knew they would come." Mary stood next to Rita. "I saw him writing letters late the other night. But I didn't know until this morning at church that he had delivered his letters to all the children in the community. Hilda Yeatts told me that."

"And don't forget those special ones who came with Benny Lester." Rosie spoke up in the midst of transferring ham biscuits from boxes onto silver serving trays. "Did you see how the children opened up to them when they arrived?"

Mary nodded. "The little ones took them by the hands and led them right out to Daniel."

"He knew the children would accept them." Rita put her arm around Mary's shoulder and squeezed her gently. Mary felt her eyes moisten. "He told me this morning before he and Isaac went out to the field that the children would come today. He said that they would be the ones whose hands would plant the sunflower seeds. I didn't know about all of this. He says it was in his dream. He says that only the children can touch the seeds. And those with childlike hearts."

Another car pulled up in the driveway, and several children spilled out of the doors and ran to Daniel, who stood with Isaac at the edge of the old corn field. Mary and Rita watched while Daniel leaned over and gave each child a bag containing seeds. He spoke to them and then sent them out with the other children who were already busy planting their seeds.

"There must be a hundred children out there, Mary. I wondered how he would do it." Rita turned when she heard the screen door open. "Oh, good." She moved toward Billy, who was balancing three pies in one hand and a cake in the other.

"Gracious!" Rosie set a covered tray of fresh vegetables down on the kitchen counter and arranged the pies and cakes along with other desserts. "Ain't nobody gonna starve today, Miz T."

"I should say not." Mary stepped into the kitchen. "We'd best get more tea made, Rosie. Rita, you and me and Billy should set up some tables out in the garden. There's going to be some hungry gardeners coming our way soon."

"We'll get some of the adults outside to help, too," Rita answered.

Mary busied herself with the task that Daniel's dream had brought her way. And never for a minute did she feel put out by it. Instead, her heart and spirit were lifted by the voices and laughter of the children he had summoned there.

Daniel dropped the sunflower seeds into a small, brown, paper bag and handed it to the little girl who knelt on both knees at his side. "Follow Isaac," he instructed, "and put a seed into the hole he makes with his stick." Daniel looked into the bright green eyes of the little girl. He smiled. "Can you do that, Molly?"

Molly's head bobbed up and down eagerly.

"Good." Daniel patted the girl on the shoulder. He pointed in the distance at the man who walked along, punching holes in the soil with the end of a long staff. It was a job Isaac had insisted upon. He had begun long before the first child had arrived, while Daniel sorted seeds and filled paper bags. "You have the last of the seeds, Molly," Daniel spoke slowly, but his words instilled the importance of her job. "The last row is yours."

Molly stood up. She held her seed bag close to her heart and looked past the children who had finished their planting and were walking back toward Daniel. She saw Isaac standing alone on the hill, waiting. "I'll plant them good, Daniel," she promised. Then she ran along the edge of the field, calling out Isaac's name.

Daniel watched her run up the hill. He stood as straight as his posture would allow and felt the warmth of the afternoon sun on his face. It was all coming together. Just like in his dream. For a moment, he closed his eyes and, in his mind, he saw the great, yellow flowers swaying in the breeze. When he opened his eyes, he was surrounded by the children and the special ones. They touched his hands, and he smiled at them. "Thank you" was all he could say. But he could not tell them that the sounds of their voices were like angels to his ears, or that the light that surrounded them was brighter than the sun. There were no words for that.

Mary Taylor could not recall a time in her life when an afternoon had passed so quickly. The voices and laughter of the children seemed to linger on the evening breeze as she walked out to the cedar swing and sat down. Rosie had gone home after the last dish was washed and dried and the leftover food put away. Billy and Rita went for a walk down to the farm pond to watch the sun set behind the pine ridge. Mary knew that walk and was happy for the young couple. She wondered if perhaps that would be the walk when Rita realized the gift she had been offered in Billy Meeks. Everyone else already knew it.

A lone mourning dove lit upon a branch of the pear tree that stood at the edge of the driveway. The bird perched motionless and silent. Mary had read that doves mated for life. She imagined that one was compelled to live, even with a broken heart. *Life goes on*, she thought. "Me without you, Frank," she said softly, sadly. But then she smiled at the memory of his laughter. *You would have enjoyed this day.* "Life. It passes so quickly." Mary looked out at the newly-planted field. She smiled again, knowing her husband would have approved of Daniel's sunflowers. Frank Taylor had always loved the colors of the world.

"Is it ready, Isaac?" Daniel asked as he opened the bag of seeds he had saved for himself.

"The circle is in the center of the field, Daniel. Just as you said it should be. There are twelve places around the center hole. Each shallow hole is three-feet apart."

"Thank you, Isaac." Daniel reached into the cloth bag he held. He stirred the seeds within the bag with his forefinger and closed his eyes.

Isaac walked away, his task completed.

The dove on the pear tree branch near the house fluttered its wings and disappeared in the time it took Mary Taylor to blink her eyes. At that precise moment, Daniel brought one seed out of his bag. He had chosen it by feel and not by sight. It was the seed he would plant in the very center of his field. The foundation of his dream. The most important seed in his possession.

An hour later, Daniel joined his grandmother in the cedar swing. The sun had fallen behind the western ridges, and faint stars began to pose in their heavenly stations.

Minutes of comfortable silence passed between the woman and the young man before Mary asked, "Where's Isaac?"

"He's gone, Mimi." Daniel did not seem sad.

Mary turned her head and saw that there was no light showing through the apartment window. "But, where…?" she began.

Daniel answered before she could finish her question. "He'll come back one day."

"Are you all right?" she asked.

Daniel nodded his head.

"What are you going to do, now that your sunflowers are planted?"

Daniel looked out toward the field. "Wait," he answered.

Mary peered over at the silhouette of the pear tree. For a moment, she wished that her husband could have been there to share the day with them. She wished that Stephen could have lived to know his son. Then she thought how wishes were like shimmering stars, so beautiful and yet so fleeting. She reached over and touched Daniel's hand. He gently squeezed her fingers and smiled. "Papa will see my flowers from heaven, Mimi." It was as if he knew her thoughts.

Mary had tears in her eyes when she agreed, "Yes, he will." She whispered, "I know he will."

When Daniel went to bed that night, he was very tired. His prayer was a short one. Just before he drifted off to sleep, he imagined the golden beauty of a sunflower bending in the breeze, its seeds falling into the hands of the children and the special ones who had come into the field that day. Their laughter echoed in his mind, and their voices, like angels, beckoned his spirit into mysterious places, and granted his body a blissful rest.

Sunflower
(The Harvest)

The month of May was like a dripping maiden stepping out of a sparkling stream, wet and shining in the sunlight. Daniel watched tender petals laden with dew steam with the morning sun's warmth. Slick earthworms stretched and slid across the pathways that led through the garden to the edge of the field, where he came to watch and wait. He was careful with his occasional doses of fertilizer. He walked slowly between the rows of tender stalks, pulling threatening weeds with his hands and tearing away creeping vines with his hoe. There was peace in the field that drew the young man to it each day. The greening of the forest that edged his field on three sides was dappled by redbud and dogwood blossoms.

Mary Taylor could watch her grandson from the cedar swing, but she could not hear the timeless songs that fell softly from his lips.

The month of June followed the dripping maiden like a sober jester. Sparing clouds teased the soil and taught young, greedy roots the art of survival. Dry, sunny days gave way to occasional showers and several drenchings. Young roots became bold and drew and stored their strength. Green stalks hardened like the bones of a child.

Daniel tended his field in the evenings, when the sun ceased its glare. Sometimes he would stand as straight as he could and face the wooded hollow, feeling the coolness that crept from its shadows and stalked the hillside.

One evening as he leaned on the handle of his hoe, he caught the twinkle of a star out of the corner of his eye. "Papa," he whispered, wondering if it was his grandfather winking at him. On another evening, he thought he heard footsteps in the soft earth behind him as he knelt to pull weeds away from the stalk of a plant. But when he turned, expecting to see his grandmother, there was no one. After that evening, Daniel never felt alone in the field again. But he was not afraid.

Mary watched from the terraces of her garden as the hillside turned green and lush. She saw the care that Daniel gave his plants. He was a determined young man, consumed by a vision only he could understand. And yet, Mary wondered if Daniel's dream was just the beginning of something they would all understand someday.

July came like a bandit in the night, waving his arms, shouting and spitting fire from his gun barrels. The sober jester paled at his audacity. There were long, hot days, and rumbling nights. The showers of May and June became downpours. Thunder echoed in the distance and pounded the ceiling of the heavens at night.

Daniel lay in his bed and marveled at the streaks of blinding light that tore apart the sky.

On a hot July afternoon, a sudden whiff of air cooled the dampness that trickled down his chest as he drove ancient tobacco sticks into the soil beside his plants with a two-pound hammer that had belonged to his grandfather. *Don't take them from me*, he pleaded silently. *I won't let them fall over and break.* Daniel carried the tobacco sticks out to the field by the armload. He pounded them into the earth and tied the plant stalks to them with bailer twine his grandfather had stored on a shelf in the shed.

"You can't tie them all, Daniel," Mary had told

him in a worried tone. "You can't save them all from what nature throws at them."

Daniel did not stop his work. *I will try*, he thought. *I will try to save them all.*

When every tobacco stick had been used, Daniel took his grandfather's handsaw into the woods and thinned the forest edges of tall saplings. He sharpened them and drove them into the soil as supports for the sunflowers that were now beginning to tower over him.

Billy Meeks was shocked and impressed when he stood at the edge of the field on the last day of July and saw that his friend had staked every sunflower stalk the children and the special ones had planted. "I would've helped you do this, Daniel." Billy was sincere, but his late offer was tinged with a measure of guilt. "Why didn't you tell me you needed help?"

The relaxed expression on Daniel's tanned face formed into the kind and gentle smile he was known for. "It is my dream, Billy." That was all he said about it.

Soon Rita joined the two young men, and together they walked quietly along the paths beneath the great mammoths. Occasionally, a bird would light on the face of a sunflower and leave it swaying amidst its still neighbors. "They're all facing the same direction," Rita suddenly noted.

Daniel stopped and looked up at the flowers.

Billy stepped up and stood beside Rita. "That's east," he pointed. "The flowers follow the sun." He lowered his hand and touched Rita's fingers. She leaned into him, and he put his arm around her waist. Billy continued, "But if they track the sun through the day, why then aren't they facing west?"

Daniel walked back to where Billy and Rita stood. He opened his lips and spoke slowly. "When they were young, they followed the sun across the sky. But the flowers are heavy now." He touched the stalk of the sunflower nearest to him. "Thick," he said. "They're getting old and stiff, like an old man."

Billy chuckled.

"God, they're beautiful." Rita was overwhelmed. "Do you feel it, Billy?" she asked, raising her hands up toward the flowers. "There is peace, a serenity here. No wonder Daniel...." She stopped, noticing that Daniel had turned and was walking on ahead of them.

"He already knows what you're feeling, Rita," Billy offered. Miz Taylor says he spends most of his days tending them."

Rita watched Daniel walk away. "It's his dream, isn't it?"

Billy knew Daniel better than most people. But aside from the obvious beauty of the sunflowers, he did not understand Daniel's fascination with them. "Yes, Rita. This is his dream, and for whatever reason, it's important to him."

August crept into the sunflower field like a slow, limping dog searching for a shady place to rest. But even in the shaded places, there was no relief from the heat. Occasional warm showers fell at night, but in the morning their wetness drifted over the landscape in an eerie, thin cloud that vanished in the hollows and lowlands as the day wore on. The ghostly apparition reappeared above the treetops along the stream bed in the evening.

The fertilizer Daniel had fed his sunflowers had done its job. The phosphorus and the potassium he had applied when the flower buds were young had rendered them hearty. When they were young, Daniel had often noticed that during the day, the flowers would follow the course of the sun across the sky. Sometimes he thought he could actually see them moving. But, once the flowers bloomed fully, they became heavy. The stalks, by that time, had become rigid, and the faces of the sunflowers locked toward the east.

One day as Daniel walked along a pathway beneath the sunflowers, he felt a need to move to the center of the field, where he, alone, had planted his seeds. Those seeds had produced the most spectacular sunflowers of all. There were eleven of them, towering three feet apart in a circle. And in the center of that circle was the twelfth one that was even greater in height. Their stalks were strong and straight, their faces fixed toward the eastern sky. All, except the face of the center flower, which hung down as if it were looking at Daniel. When he saw it, he felt as if a light was shining through his body. The sounds of nature around him gathered in intensity so that he covered his ears and dropped to his knees. Then, there was a deepening silence. And out of that silence came a heartbeat that Daniel recognized as his own. Visions began to flicker in his mind. Faces he knew, places he had been, and things he had done. The dream. Sunflowers — fields of them, all over the world. Words he could not say. A Bible with its pages blowing in the wind. The face of a woman. And then nothing. There was silence before a familiar voice spoke his name.

"Daniel. Open your eyes."

Daniel opened his eyes and lifted his face. "Isaac," he said. "Where have you been?"

The old man walked around the circle of sunflowers and reached out his hand. "Stand," he said as Daniel took his hand. "I have been away, tending to some matters."

"I knew you would come back." Daniel felt groggy and shook his head.

"Steady now, son." Isaac touched the young man on his shoulder.

"I saw a…." Daniel struggled to form the word he wanted to say.

Isaac already knew. "You saw her face, didn't you?" He looked directly into Daniel's eyes.

Daniel nodded his head. "Yes. Who is she?"

"You'll know soon." Isaac stepped away from Daniel and turned to walk away.

"Where are you going?" Daniel did not want Isaac to leave.

"I won't be far away." He smiled. "I think you

know that." He turned and began to whistle as he disappeared into the shadows.

"But when will she come?" Daniel called. He followed his friend, but could not catch up with him.

"Sleep on the flower that bends to you, Daniel. Then you will know." Isaac's voice trailed his disappearance into the shadows.

Daniel stopped walking and rubbed his eyes with his handkerchief. When he looked again for Isaac, the old man was gone. *The flower that bends to you.* Daniel repeated Isaac's words in his mind. He turned and walked back to the center of the field to where the face of one sunflower tilted downward. "Sleep on the sunflower, and you will know the truth." Daniel recalled the words of his grandmother. He reached into his pocket and brought out the knife his grandfather had given him. "The truth," Daniel said softly as he stepped closer and touched the rigid stalk. For a minute Daniel closed his eyes. He could feel the strength, the very life of the sunflower plant come through his hand. A subtle force moved up his arm and seemed to flow through his body. He rested his forehead against the stalk, and the breeze that rustled the leaves of the giant flowers around him came to his ears like the whisperings of angels. Thin, worded pages turned in his mind—words he could not say. Visions. A hand reached out to him from a misty forest. The sun. A face. Her face. And then he heard a voice. "Sleep on the flower, Daniel." It was a young woman's voice, warm and gentle. Daniel opened his eyes. He felt weak, but he knew what he had to do.

Slowly he stepped back while pulling down the stalk. And when he pressed the face of the sunflower against his heart, he cut it free. At that moment, there was a nearby flutter of wings, and a sway over the flowers in the field that moved like a long swell in the ocean. Daniel put away his knife, then stood there admiring the sunflower he held in his hands. It was larger than all the rest. Its seeds were many, and its yellow petals flamed with beauty. Daniel could not help but know that there was a purpose in his possessing it. Without guilt, he walked out of the field.

"I saw you working in your sunflowers today." Mary pushed the bowl of new potatoes closer to Daniel's dinner plate. She had noticed his lack of an appetite. He was quieter than usual, too. Daniel showed no interest in her not-so-subtle offering.

"What is Rosie going to say when she sees that you didn't even touch those potatoes?" Mary asked without scolding. "They are one of your favorites," she added as she pulled the bowl back over to her plate and placed two small slices beside her green beans.

"I'm not hungry, Mimi." Daniel had hardly touched his food. He pushed his plate away, leaned forward, his elbows on the table, and rested his chin on his hands. For a minute, he looked intently at his grandmother.

Mary knew the look. It had not changed since he was a little boy. She laid her fork down and touched her lips with her napkin. Age had been such a thief to her eyesight. But she could still somehow feel the intensity of his stare. "A penny for your thoughts," she said, wishing she could see his dark, brown eyes. They would be looking directly into hers, reading her mood. He was good at that—a real master at knowing when to pose a question.

"Did you ever sleep with a sunflower under your pillow?" he finally asked.

Mary wondered what was behind Daniel's question. She knew from the experience of raising him that there was a reason for it. She also knew that the reason would be forthcoming, though probably at a much later time. She raised her eyebrows and shook her head. "No, I can't say that I ever actually did that." She smiled at a memory. "My mother told me that she did it occasionally to know the truth of a matter. But I think that she might have been playing with me."

"What if she was telling you the truth, Mimi?"

Mary smiled. "Then that would answer the question as to how it was almost impossible to get away with anything when she was around."

"She knew things?" Daniel asked.

"Oh, yes. She knew plenty." Mary reached over and patted Daniel on the back of his hand. "Is something troubling you?" There was concern in her tone. "Has something happened that you want to tell me about?"

Daniel shook his head. His grandmother knew not to take the matter any further. He would talk when the time was right.

"You remind me of my mother, Daniel."

"I do?"

"Yes. You have her dark, brown eyes." Mary smiled, but there was a sadness in her that she could no longer see into those eyes. "You have her heart."

There was a noise out on the patio as Rosie set a box of old clothing on the slate table and began sorting. "Daniel," she called. "Can you bring that last box down from the apartment? I'm afraid your old Rosie's legs have done played out on her."

Daniel got up and walked out onto the patio. Mary followed him outside.

"What are you doing, Rosie?" he asked while looking at the assortment of old clothing.

Rosie folded a worn flannel shirt that had belonged to Frank Taylor. She placed it atop a pile of shirts much too large for Daniel to wear. "Your Mimi wants to give these to the Goodwill. If you see anything you want, you'd better grab it."

Daniel looked at the clothes, but did not seem interested.

"Rosie, you take some of those better shirts of Frank's home for Henry, if he can use them." Mary folded a white and yellow gingham sundress that she had worn as a young woman. She remembered that Frank had often said she looked pretty in that dress.

"My goodness, Miz T." Rosie eyed the sundress. "You sure was a little thing when you was young." The big woman looked over at Daniel and winked. "Your Mimi ain't much bigger now, is she?"

Daniel smiled and then turned around and headed toward the apartment. "I'll bring the box down," he said.

When he was out of earshot, Rosie talked freely. "There's something on that young man's mind, Miz T. You know it, don't you?" Rosie had known Daniel all his life and was more like an aunt to him than one who was there to help around the house.

"He almost told me something at the supper table tonight," Mary confessed. She decided she could not part with the old sundress, and she set it to the side. "Have you noticed anything odd?"

Rosie put one hand on her hip and touched her chin with the thumb of her other hand. She looked up and puckered her lips. "Well, let's see now, Miz T. He has this dream about a sunflower field. Then he goes out and buys out Forrest Meeks' supply of sunflowers. Then he somehow pulls a stranger outta nowhere to get that old tractor running, and has him to get the field ready for a planting." Rosie sighed and rubbed her chin. She cocked an eye over at Mary and continued. "Then he has all the children of Hopeful and them poor less-fortunates to come up here and plant all them seeds. Won't let no adult even touch a seed. He tends to them flowers like they was something real special. He even stakes and ties each one so they won't blow down. He disappears in that field every day and won't leave it, 'cept to eat, sleep, and go to work." Rosie looked at Mary and shook her head.

She reached in the box and pulled out another one of Frank's old shirts and began to fold it. "Before I set dinner on the table, I laid his shirts and socks on the foot of his bed, and you wouldn't believe what's layin' there on his pillow."

"What is it?" Mary could not imagine.

"He's done cut one of them sunflowers and brung it in there and laid it down, and for what, I don't know. But it'd dwarf one of your big cherry pies, and that ain't no lie. Biggest sunflower I ever seen." Rosie took a long breath and shook her head. "But, uh-uh, Miz T. Aside from a few little things somebody else might think was a bit peculiar, I ain't seen nothin' odd. How 'bout you?" Rosie stopped to rest her mouth and waited for Mary to reply to her observations. She was not really surprised when there was nothing but silence in return.

There was not one good story on the television news that night. Mary watched in disgust as one report after another told of house foreclosures, lost jobs, and greedy bank executives.

Daniel walked into the den as the death count was given in connection with a devastating earthquake in Italy. A man was shown weeping for his wife and children who were buried beneath the rubble that used to be their home. The man's anguished face was streaked with dirt and tears. Daniel closed his eyes and sighed. "I'm tired, Mimi." His comment was a seldom-heard admission.

Mary lifted her hand from the armrest of her chair and squeezed Daniel's hand with her fingers. "You go on to bed and don't worry about these things." She knew the news stories bothered him immensely. "The world is in God's hands."

Daniel opened his eyes as the face of an eight-year-old girl appeared on the screen. The report was grim. The girl had disappeared a few days earlier while playing in the street outside her home. Now it was feared hers was the body found in a suitcase at the edge of a swamp.

"Oh, no." Mary put her hand to her mouth.

Daniel looked down at his grandmother and shook his head. He bent down and kissed her on the cheek. "Good night, Mimi," was all he said.

Mary pushed the "off" button on her television remote. She watched Daniel leave the den and, for a while, she stared at the blank television screen. She felt as if she wanted to pray, but she did not even know where to begin. Instead, she picked up her Bible from the side table and found her place beside a red, silk bookmark she had closed the pages on the night before. She began reading at Matthew 6. The first verses brought cherished memories of her husband to mind. Always doing for others, he had laid away his gifts in heaven. She knew that. Soon she came to the verses she needed. *Your Father knoweth what things ye have need of, before ye ask him.* Mary closed her eyes and as her lips moved with heartfelt and silent words, a tear coursed down her cheek.

Daniel had never felt more tired than he did that night. The visions he had seen in the sunflower field were still clear in his mind. The appearance of Isaac had convinced him of something he already suspected. Isaac was not just a good-natured vagabond passing through Hopeful. There was a purpose in his presence. Daniel was sure of it. The old man somehow knew the visions in his head. "Sleep on the flower that bends to you." Daniel remembered the words of his friend. Isaac knew the face of the woman Daniel had seen in his dream. "Sleep on the flower," she had said. Daniel repeated the words. He lay down on his bed, and suddenly the pictures he had seen on the television news glared in his memory. He winced and shook his head. Then he reached his hand beneath his pillow and felt the soft petals of the sunflower he had brought in from the field. It calmed him immediately.

Slowly his mind began to drift. A prayer, selfless and true, spilled from his heart and came as a whisper on his lips. It fell upon the breeze that swept past Daniel's open window, and soon his whispered prayer brushed the great and beautiful flowers that slumbered in the black and white world of the night. Clouds parted and, for a moment, the moon and the stars paled in the presence of a heavenly light that shown down upon Daniel's field. The creatures of the night were silenced. Even the gurgling stream that circled the lower boundary of the field became still.

The sunflowers raised their faces toward the light. And in those moments, a prayer was answered, and a dream began to unravel into a truth that would touch the hearts of men all over the world.

When Rosie Holman pulled her car into its place next to Mary Taylor's Buick the next morning, she noticed the woman sitting alone on the cedar swing on the terrace above the garden. Concerned, the big woman got out of her car and approached her dear friend.

"Miz T?" Rosie was close behind Mary before she called her name. She walked around to the right side of the woman and stood watching her far-away gaze. "Miz T?" she asked again. "Are you all right?"

Mary did not look at Rosie when she spoke. "My eyes have become so bad now that I can hardly see the flowers, Rosie. I can't even see my grandson's eyes anymore." When she turned her face, Rosie could see her sad expression. She felt an immediate compassion for her friend. Putting down her handbag, Rosie walked over and stood behind Mary with her hands on the frail woman's shoulders. "Oh, now, Miz T," she consoled. "Don't you fret 'bout that. You know that me and Daniel will always be here for you. We'll be your eyes."

Mary quietly reached back and touched Rosie's hand. "Last night he was troubled, and I tried to look in his eyes. I couldn't even see them."

"Well, let me just tell you somethin', sweet lady." Rosie gently rubbed Mary's shoulders with her fingers. "That young man's eyes are still just as brown as chocolate and full of life and promise. Don't you worry none 'bout Daniel. He ain't got no problem he can't overcome. And I never seen someone with more faith in the Lord than him. Wish I had, 'cause the world sure needs the faithful now. People have done fallen into a den of troubles all over, and I fear for their souls. But Daniel, he ain't got no troubles. He'd walk out of that den of troubles and lead the way for anyone who's got just a speck of what he's made of." Rosie patted Mary's shoulders. "Don't you worry none 'bout that boy. He's special, but not for things he can't do."

Mary agreed. "You're right about that, Rosie. But I'd love to see his eyes again. His handsome face."

"I know, Miz T. I know you would."

A butterfly darted out of a cluster of pink and white azaleas. Mary tried to follow its path through the garden with her eyes. "This eye affliction allows me to see the beauty that surrounds something but not the source of it."

Rosie thought for a minute. "It's kind of like a faith in the Lord, ma'am. We can see the beauty of his promise, but not him."

Mary smiled. "You keep it up, Rosie, and I'm going to take you to church so you can give the preacher a run for his pulpit."

Both women laughed.

"No, Miz T. I wouldn't be much at no church. I come closest to it right here with you and Daniel and these beautiful flowers you done tended to all these years."

Rosie walked away from the swing and picked up her handbag. The morning sun felt warm on her back as she straightened up and looked out toward the sunflower field. She watched as a small flock of birds swooped into the field. She started toward the patio, then something else caught her eye. "Is Daniel over there in the sunflowers, Miz T?"

"No." Mary looked over at Rosie. "He's been tired lately, and I didn't wake him this morning."

Rosie put her handbag down on the ground and put both hands on her hips. She leaned forward and strained her eyes. "Well, somebody just walked out of that field and is coming this way." Rosie took a few steps forward.

"Can you tell who it might be?" Mary asked while trying to detect movement.

"No," answered Rosie. "But whoever it is just

walked into those big sunflowers Daniel planted in the old garden. I can see 'em walkin' up the row, but I can't...." Rosie stopped.

"What do you see, Rose?" Mary stood up and stared at the old garden site. She could see the towering yellow flowers but could not focus on any movement.

Rosie walked out in front of Mary, her hands still on both hips. "Well, I ain't never...." she began.

"What, Rosie? Who is it?" Mary was anxious.

Rosie looked back at Mary. "Miz T," she said in a quiet voice. "You might want to sit back down. We got us a visitor the likes of nothin' I've ever seen, comin' outta no garden."

"Who is it?" Mary sat down again.

"She's comin' closer. Come on out," she coaxed.

"You said 'she,' Rosie," Mary repeated. "Is it a woman?"

Rosie could not believe her eyes. She blinked them and then rubbed one with her thumb. "Come on, child," she urged softly. "What are you doing out here like this? Are you lost? What happened?"

Mary heard Rosie's questions, but there were no answers. "Rosie?" She waited.

"Miz T." Rosie stood still but did not look back as she spoke. "We got a young lady here at the edge of the garden."

"Ask her name, Rosie."

"What's your name, honey?" Rosie moved closer to the young woman. She noticed that there was no sign of alarm on the woman's face.

But still there was no response.

"She won't tell her name, Miz T." Rosie reached out her hand, and the young woman walked closer to her. "That's it, honey. You come to Rosie." She waited. "You must be lost, child."

"Rosie?" Mary was incredulous. "Tell me something!"

Rosie spoke softly. "Well, this young lady is as pretty as the morning is and as naked as a raindrop."

"Naked?" Mary's surprise filled her voice.

"Ain't even got no shoes on, Miz T."

By now the young woman was standing close in front of Rosie. But when she looked over and saw Mary, she walked unashamedly over to her and stood as if she were waiting for the older woman to recognize her.

"Look at the butterflies all around her." Rosie had noticed several on her head and shoulders, but now there was a fluttering frenzy of colorful wings around her.

"I see them!" Mary answered excitedly. "I can see the colors of their wings."

The young woman put out her hand and, without hesitation, Mary touched her fingers.

"Isaac had butterflies around him all the time, too," Rosie offered as she stepped closer to the young woman.

The young woman's fingers were warm. Mary could sense she was not afraid.

"What is your name?" Mary asked as she strained to see a face.

For a few seconds there was silence. And then

Mary heard Daniel's voice. "Sunflower," he said. "Her name is Sunflower." He walked around the swing and handed Rosie the yellow and white gingham dress that had belonged to his grandmother. "Can you help her with this, Rosie?"

Rosie took the dress and walked over to the girl.

Daniel looked for a moment into the darkness of the young woman's brown eyes, and then he looked away respectfully while Rosie slipped the sundress over her head and straightened it around her hips.

"Sunflower." Mary stood up and repeated the name. "Do you know her, Daniel?" She looked at her grandson and then back at the girl.

"I knew she was coming." Daniel could feel Sunflower's gaze upon him as he answered his grandmother. He met it with a smile.

"Daniel." Sunflower said his name as if it were a precious memory.

Mary noticed. "Where did you come from?" she asked.

The girl looked back at the field of swaying sunflowers and pointed. "There," she said, "and there." She looked at Daniel.

Rosie opened her mouth but could not utter a word. She did not even know how to begin.

"Are you alone?" Mary asked in a sympathetic tone. "Are you lost?"

"I am by myself, but I am not alone," Sunflower answered. She looked around and saw that she was surrounded by a garden with colors both rich and pale. A single dove came into the garden and perched in the dappled sunlight of a vine-covered arbor. No one else seemed to notice it.

Sunflower heard the soft flutter of the dove's wings. "I am not lost," she said. She looked down and seemed to notice for the first time the dress that clung loosely to her body. She touched the fabric with her fingers. "It is beautiful," she said.

Mary could see that the dress fit the young woman perfectly. And although she could not focus her vision on the face of the strange visitor, she could sense a beauty about her.

Rosie could see the details of which Mary could only imagine. The girl Daniel called Sunflower was of medium height, and although she was rather thin, the curves of her femininity fit well the mold of her physique. Her skin was olive, and her hands were delicate. She stood straight. There was confidence in her posture. The slightest breeze could rearrange the long, silky blonde hair that draped over her collarbone and swept down her back. A fairy princess would have coveted such golden locks.

Rosie was intrigued by the presence of Sunflower, but she was not afraid. "Miz T," Rosie said, clearing her throat and shifting her eyes toward Daniel as she addressed his grandmother. "I'll take Sunflower in for a glass of water, while you and Daniel talk."

Mary nodded. She touched Sunflower on the arm and urged her to follow Rosie to the back of the house. "Yes, Rosie. It's warm already this morning, and I'm sure our new friend could use a drink of water and perhaps something to eat."

Sunflower smiled. She understood. It would take a while for them to understand. But not Daniel. He already knew to trust her. Her dark eyes found his as she turned and walked by him. And in a glance, she could see that he was not afraid.

A warm breeze oozed through the garden as Sunflower followed Rosie into the house.

Daniel stood there and watched the screen door close behind them. He waited for the silence that had always come before his grandmother would scold him as a boy. But there was no silence. And there were no questioning looks from her.

Mary walked over to Daniel and caressed his face with her hands. "I love you, Daniel. And I know that something is going on here. The dream, and your field of sunflowers. Isaac and all those children. And now this girl."

Daniel lowered his face toward his grandmother. She kissed his forehead. "Promise me that when it's time, you will tell me what is happening."

Daniel put his arms around the woman who had raised him. "I will, Mimi." He looked up at the apartment window above the garage, then back at his grandmother. "Can she sleep there?" he asked.

Although Mary had been cautious and protective of Daniel all his life, her fear for him had somehow diminished with the arrival of Sunflower. As odd as the young woman's appearance seemed, her mere presence was calming to Mary. There were questions to be answered, naturally, but that morning beside the cedar swing in the flower garden Mary's answer to Daniel's request seemed more pertinent than the things she did not yet know. "Yes, she can stay," Mary heard herself say.

Daniel smiled. "She's good, Mimi."

"Right now your belief in her is good enough for me." Mary looked toward the kitchen door. "People will be asking where she came from. What are you prepared to tell them?"

Daniel answered calmly as though he had already considered his grandmother's concern. "I'm not going to tell them anything," he answered. His dark eyes were fixed upon the sunflower field until he turned his head toward his grandmother. "She will."

For a moment, Mary felt as though Daniel's soul was seeping through his eyes. She could feel it. There was a confidence she had never recognized in his voice. There was something within him that reached beyond anything she could have ever hoped for him. A deep-seated-wisdom.

"Miz T." Rosie's voice broke the spell of the moment, and both Mary and Daniel looked at the woman who was standing with one foot out the kitchen door. "You ought to see this girl eat!" Rosie waved her hand for the two to come in. "I mean it's like she ain't had nothin' to eat for a month of Sundays." Rosie stepped back into the house. The screen door slammed behind her.

Mary started down the shallow steps that led onto the footpath to the patio. "Let's go see that your friend doesn't eat us out of house and home, Daniel."

Daniel glanced back at the sunflower field before he followed his grandmother into the house.

"Where are they, Rosie?" Mary rubbed the sleep from her eyes as she walked groggily out onto the patio. It was mid-afternoon.

"How was your nap, Miz T?" Rosie asked without looking up from her flower-arranging project. "I guess you didn't hear the truck start up, then." She snipped the stem of a rose and filled a gap in the arrangement with its blood-red petals.

Mary paused by the table and admired Rosie's work. Then she walked to the corner of the patio and stood in a sunny spot, her bare feet gleaning the warmth from the sun on the slate. "They went into town?" she asked.

Rosie stood up and placed the flower vase in the center of the slate-top table. She turned the vase a few times and then walked over and joined Mary in the afternoon sun. "Daniel wanted to take Sunflower over to the café to meet Lucy and Rita, and then they was gonna go by the corner store to pick up a few things for supper." Rosie chuckled and fanned the gnats away from her face with her hands. She rested both hands on her hips and shook her head. "I ain't seen a young lady eat so much and be so thin in my life."

Mary recalled the table of food Rosie had prepared for Sunflower, and how the tip of the girl's nose was white with cake icing when she and Daniel had come in earlier. "Lord only knows the last time she ate. What do you think, Rosie?"

Rosie rubbed her chin with her forefinger and thumb before answering. "I don't know, Miz T, but she ain't shy. Pretty as can be. I couldn't hardly get her to wear no shoes. Finally coaxed her into wearing a pair of your white cloth yard shoes. But she walked in them like it won't natural for her." Rosie scratched her temple and walked back to the patio table. She sat down and pulled out a chair for Mary. "It's a mystery, all right, Miz T. I'd almost say she's a lost child. Maybe even a little bit wild. But she's reserved enough to show you she's got some discipline. There's just somethin' 'bout her. She comes up here without anything to show who she is and, in a minute, we're treatin' her like a member of the family. One part of me wants to tell you to contact the sheriff 'bout her, but then a voice in me says not to." Rosie leaned back in her chair and began running her fingers along the stitches in her work apron. "I don't know what to tell you, Miz T. But I don't think she's nothin' but good. Lost maybe. But good."

"Daniel knew she was coming." Mary spoke as she pulled the day's mail from beside the flower arrangement. "He knew her name."

"Do you think Sunflower is really her name?" Rosie retrieved a small, thin pocketknife from her apron pocket, opened it, and pushed it across the table.

Mary studied the address on a small envelope. She blinked her eyes several times and then slit the top of the envelope with the razor-sharp blade of Rosie's knife. She fumbled with the card inside. "Yes, I do think it's her name. It fits her well enough."

Rosie watched the concentration on Mary's face as she opened the small card in her hands. "Well, I reckon it does fit her, seein' as how all we know about her is that she come out of that flower field." Rosie leaned forward and put her hands on the table. "You all right, Miz T?" she asked. "Is somethin' the matter?"

Mary blinked her eyes and then rubbed them with her fingers. She put the card down on the table and looked at it without squinting.

Rosie watched in silent puzzlement as the woman urgently opened a bill and spread it out on the table in front of her. "Twenty-three dollars and fifty-eight cents." Mary tapped the bill with her forefinger. "That's for the bird feed Daniel picked up last month from Forrest Meeks' store." There was guarded excitement in the tone of her voice.

Rosie studied Mary's face. "How did you…?" she began.

"Read it?" Mary finished Rosie's question. She read aloud a hand-written note from John Grayling's wife, Jane, thanking her for a pecan pie she had sent over by Daniel the week before. Mary dropped the note and looked across the table. "I can see your face, Rosie. I mean I can see your whole face—not just the perimeters, but your nose and mouth, eyes, and…everything!"

Rosie did not know what to say. For the past few years, Mary Taylor's eyesight had been going bad.

There had been two unsuccessful surgeries to improve her macular degeneration before Mary had finally resigned herself to the inevitable. And now, she could see? "What in the world, Miz T?" Rosie stood up and grasped Mary's hands. Tears were beginning to flow from Mary's eyes as she stood up.

"I know." Mary patted Rosie on the back of her hand. Then she let go of the big woman and walked along the narrow pathway that led through her garden. The flowers never looked more beautiful to her than at that moment. She touched certain ones as she passed, and when she came to the end of the pathway, she bent over and inhaled the fragrance of the roses she and her husband had set along a rail fence at the edge of the yard. When she raised up again, she looked beyond the garden and saw, for the first time, Daniel's sunflowers. Her vision was clear. They were spectacular in the afternoon sun. "I know," she whispered.

Lucy Wenby filled two glasses with sweet tea and set the tea pitcher down on the counter beside the straw dispenser. She handed two straws to Daniel and leaned back in her high-back chair behind the counter.

"I like it," she said with a smile. Lucy repeated the young woman's name. "Sunflower." She looked over at Daniel and winked. "Where have you been keeping her, Daniel?"

Daniel watched as Sunflower struggled to remove the plastic wrapper from her straw. He reached over and handed her his already-opened straw and took hers.

Lucy watched him tear the top of the plastic with his fingers and remove the straw. He pushed it down into his tea glass and stirred the contents. There was a hint of a smile on his lips, but no attempt on his part to answer her.

"I came out of the field." Sunflower stirred her iced tea with her straw the same as Daniel had.

Lucy could see the girl was mimicking his moves. "The field?" Lucy repeated.

"Yes. The sunflower field." Sunflower watched Daniel suck tea through his straw. Then she lowered her head and placed her own straw between her lips. The sensation of the cold sweetness in her mouth brought a smile to her face.

Lucy thought Sunflower was like a child discovering something new. She wondered if the girl was special. Daniel had lots of friends in Special Olympics. She did not know them all. "It's good, isn't it?" Lucy stood up and leaned forward, resting her elbows on the counter. "So, you've been helping Daniel with his sunflowers?" Lucy had become intrigued. She watched Daniel as she posed her question. He was looking down into his tea glass.

Sunflower shook her head from side to side. "No, not really." She cut her eyes over at Daniel and smiled.

Daniel looked up at Lucy, but did not speak.

The woman knew him well enough to know he was not going to offer any explanation. "Well, Sunflower, you have a beautiful name, and I'm glad Daniel brought you by to see me today."

"Thank you, Lucy." Sunflower finished her tea and pushed her empty glass forward as she raised her eyebrows. "Could I have some more of that?"

Lucy filled the girl's glass. "You can have all you want, honey. It's on the house."

"Do you like my dress, Lucy?" Sunflower stood up and looked down at the light gingham dress Rosie had put on her. She pressed the cool fabric against her flat stomach with her fingers. "It feels good on my skin."

Lucy smiled at Sunflower's seeming innocence. "And you look absolutely stunning in it," she offered.

"It was Mary's when she was young," Sunflower said as she returned to her stool next to Daniel. She drank some more tea, then asked, "Where is Rita?"

"Rita was tired after the lunch crowd left today. She's upstairs taking a nap." Lucy had wanted to awaken Rita when Daniel came in with his new friend, but she knew that Rita was exhausted.

"Daniel has told me about her. I want to talk with her soon." Sunflower seemed genuinely interested.

Lucy was not sure how to take Sunflower's persistent nature. Some people would have deemed her forward. But Lucy was not so sure that she was. She wondered if perhaps curious would better describe the girl's nature. But there was something else, also. Lucy could somehow feel it, but would have difficulty explaining it if she had to.

The front door of the café suddenly opened, and Billy Meeks walked in. "Hey, Daniel," he called from the door. "Lucy." Billy approached the three people at the counter.

"Hi, Billy." Daniel shook Billy's hand.

"Where have you been, Daniel?" Billy removed his cap and winked at Lucy. "Your grandma says you've been in that sunflower field every day. I'll bet those flowers are a sight by now. I've been meaning to come up, but Dad has me out on the road these days selling and delivering. That job I talked to you about at the loading bay is a sure thing, if you want it."

Daniel's eyes lit up. "Really?"

Billy chuckled. "Yeah. Dad can't do that on his own, and I'm on the road three days a week. Could you handle Tuesdays and Thursdays to start out?"

"When do I start?" Daniel was excited.

"How about next week?" Billy had already talked with his dad about the prospect of hiring Daniel on a part-time basis. "Say 'bout nine to three."

Daniel agreed. "That sounds good, Billy. Thanks."

Billy tipped his head and slapped his cap against his thigh. "Good," he said. "Now, who is this?" He looked at the girl sitting on the stool in front of him.

"This is Sunflower," Daniel answered. "She came from my sunflower field."

Billy laughed. "Well, then the name is appropriate, isn't it?" He looked at Daniel, then at the brown-eyed girl with the fetching smile. "Hello, Sunflower."

"Hello, Billy Meeks. Daniel has told me about you."

"Oh, he has?"

"Yes. He says you are in love with Rita, but she does not know it. And you want to marry her."

Billy's jaw dropped. He was speechless. His eyes darted from Sunflower to Daniel to Lucy and then back to Sunflower.

"Well, I...." he began hesitantly.

Sunflower did not wait for him to continue. "Do you want some tea? It is cold and sweet and Lucy says it's on the house." The girl looked over at Lucy and caught the woman's closed-mouth smile. "Right, Lucy?"

"Of course it is." Lucy went along with Sunflower's show of hospitality. "Sit down, Billy, and have a glass of tea while I get your soup and sandwich ready." Lucy reached under the counter and brought up a glass, which she filled with ice, then tea. "Excuse me, kids." Lucy disappeared around the corner into the kitchen, carrying her smile with her. "It'll be ready in a few minutes, Billy," she called back. "Rita's resting."

Billy sat down on a stool beside Sunflower. He scratched his jaw. Then he adjusted himself on the stool, leaned forward, turned his head and spoke. "Well, Daniel, I didn't know it was so obvious."

Daniel smiled.

"I guess everyone knows it except for her." Billy

rubbed the counter top with the palms of his hands.

"She knows, too," Daniel said. He looked at Sunflower.

Billy shrugged. "I'm afraid to tell her because she's been through so much, and all. I guess I'm scared that she won't want to give me a chance to show her what I'm made of." Billy looked at Sunflower. He was comfortable enough with her. He did not know why, though. She just did not seem like a stranger, or someone he could not trust. "Daniel knows I'd marry her in a minute, if she'd have me. And I'd be a good daddy to her baby, if…."

"If she would give you a chance?" Sunflower knew Billy Meeks was feeling more than he could have explained.

"Yeah." Billy tapped his fingers on the counter.

"Fear is a hard emotion to conquer, Billy." Sunflower's dark eyes somehow gave credence to her words. "Especially when the fear is deep-rooted. Rita's fear is of rejection. It has affected her self-worth to the point where she cannot believe you or anyone could love her."

"How do you know so much about her?" Billy was curious. "How can you know?"

"I know the human condition." Sunflower looked directly into Billy's eyes. "Daniel has told me a little about Rita's past. It is not hard for me to understand someone. Believe me, it is not."

Billy was at ease with Sunflower right from the start. There was a freedom about her, a sense of wisdom that radiated from her, and urged a confidence he thought he lacked. "I'd like to just tell her the way I feel. Maybe I can do that."

"Do not force it. And when you do tell her, be careful that your words express your heart. The rest will be up to her."

Billy was quiet for a minute. He sipped his tea and thought about how he could tell Rita what was in his heart. "Maybe we can all do something together," he suggested. "A movie, maybe?"

"I've never seen a movie." Sunflower looked over at Daniel. "But I like stories. Would you want me to tell a story?"

"So you're a storyteller, then?" Billy was interested.

"I know a lot of stories." Sunflower finished her tea and pushed her glass away. "Would you want me to tell a story to your friends, Daniel?"

Daniel loved Sunflower's voice and her eagerness. Instinctively he knew there would be a purpose in anything she cared to share with him or anyone else. He could feel her eyes upon him. She knew his answer before he even voiced it.

"Bring Rita up to the house tomorrow night," he said, looking past the girl, at Billy. "Come before dark so you can see the flowers."

Lucy appeared at the kitchen door with Billy's soup and sandwich. "Here you go, Billy." She placed the bowl and plate in front of him, then refilled his tea glass. "More tea, honey?" She looked at Sunflower.

"No, thank you, Lucy." She smiled. "Daniel is going to show me the town." She turned and slid off her stool.

126

Lucy picked up Sunflower's glass and wiped the counter with a small towel. "There's not much to see in Hopeful, but at least you've got good company." She smiled at Daniel.

Sunflower walked toward the door. "Goodbye," she said as she stepped out into the afternoon sunlight.

Daniel followed her outside. "Tell Rita 'hi,'" he called back before the glass door closed behind him.

It was quiet in Lucy's Café for a while after Sunflower and Daniel left. Billy ate his lunch and thought about what he wanted to say to Rita.

Lucy replenished the tables and counter with napkins. She made sure everything was properly arranged for the usual customers who would come by for their mid-afternoon coffees and teas. A fresh carrot cake with vanilla icing, a cheesecake, and assorted cookies were brought out of the kitchen and displayed under a glass covering on the counter. Billy eyed the carrot cake until Lucy cut him a well-portioned slice and placed it on his empty sandwich plate. "Thanks, Lucy." Billy scooped the icing off the top of his dessert with the tip of his spoon.

"Daniel said she came out of his sunflower field." Billy looked up from his dessert as he spoke.

Lucy watched the fan blades from the ceiling units move in unison above the tables of her café. "I know."

Billy tasted the icing on his spoon and waited for Lucy to continue.

"What do you think?" Lucy posed her question without taking her eyes off the fan blades.

"What? About the cake or the girl?" Billy licked his top lip and grinned.

"The girl." Lucy's tone was serious.

Billy put his spoon down beside his plate. He puckered his lips, then relaxed his face and looked up at the woman. "I don't know what to think, Lucy. But I've never known Daniel to make anything up like that."

"There is something about her that just sets you at ease," Lucy offered.

"Yeah. Exactly," Billy agreed. He stood up and placed his cake on a napkin. "Gotta go." He turned away from the counter. "Tell Rita I'll be by around supper time."

Lucy walked around the end of the counter and followed the young man to the door. "I'll tell her, Billy."

Billy opened the door and paused. "You know, it won't be long before her baby comes, Lucy."

Lucy's expression was caring. "The doctor told her it would be a week to ten days into November."

Billy bit inside his upper lip. His eyes went from the sidewalk to back inside the café and then to Lucy. "I want her to marry me, Lucy. I want her child to have a daddy. It's a hard world out there. I just know I can be what she needs—what they need."

Lucy touched Billy on the arm. She felt her eyes moisten as she tried to hold back her emotions. "You're a good young man, Billy Meeks," she said softly. "And I don't doubt your sincerity at all."

"Do you think Rita does?"

Lucy sighed. "I think Rita is wrestling with a past that has left her scarred and afraid. Her reluctance to give in to her heart has a lot to do with her self-esteem. But I think she loves you, Billy. I really do. She's just too afraid to say it. Afraid that you'll go away."

"You know I wouldn't go away."

"Yes, I do know that. And one day, so will she."

"I pray for that day, Lucy." Billy looked away, but Lucy could detect the emotion in his voice.

"You keep on praying, Billy. Don't stop." Lucy watched Billy amble down the sidewalk to where his truck was parked. It was a splendid, cloudless August day. The heat from the sidewalk warmed her feet through the thin soles of her flat summer sandals. As Billy started his truck's engine and pulled away, she noticed that there were only a handful of cars parked alongside the street. There were no people to be seen. For a moment, Lucy remembered a bustling little town, with colorful storefronts. That seemed so long ago. Now things were quiet in Hopeful. There were more vacant stores than she could ever recall. People just did not come out much at all, especially lately, with the news media playing up the threat of a flu pandemic. Lucy shook her head as she raised her face to the sun. *There are no flowers on the sidewalks anymore,* Lucy thought. *I should have put out some flower pots this summer. There's no color.* Lucy turned to step back into the café when, suddenly, a movement caught her attention just inside the door. There was a butterfly fluttering back and forth along the café window. Lucy had not seen the butterfly enter the store and had no idea how long it had been inside. She marveled at its beauty. Its black and yellow wings seemed larger than most she had seen before, and the blue and red highlights were stunning. Lucy opened the door wide and stood to the side. "What in the world brought such a beautiful creature as you into our flowerless little town?" she asked aloud. The swallow tail skipped into the stream of cool air that circulated the interior of the café and fluttered its wings as it darted past Lucy's face and into the outside heat. "Go find a flower, pretty one." Lucy stepped inside and pulled the door closed behind her. Then she stood there watching until the butterfly flew out of sight.

For hours after they left Lucy's Café, Daniel and Sunflower explored the town of Hopeful and its surrounding streets and houses. Daniel even drove her out to the Grayling's dairy farm, where old silage bins still stood like war-damaged sentinels in the middle of ragged, neglected fields.

"John used to have hundreds of milk cows on this place," Daniel told her. "But he got old, and his children didn't want to farm." Daniel parked his truck at the edge of a narrow bridge at Sunflower's request. She wanted to walk in the creek below. Knowing his limited balance, Daniel was hesitant to take off his shoes to join her.

Sunflower urged him into the water. "I'll walk beside you," she said as she offered him her hand. "I won't let you fall."

Daniel had not walked in water since he was a boy, and his grandfather had helped him along. The cool water and sandy bottom felt good on his feet. At first, he was unsure of his steps, but as he progressed upstream without stumbling, he became more confident.

"Let's sit here," Sunflower finally said as they made a turn in the wide, shallow stream. The small, sandy beach she chose was shaded by a thick tree canopy, joined by winding wild grapevines. The gurgle of the water as it slurped around mossy stones added to the coolness of the place.

Daniel watched Sunflower sit down in the sand. She lay back. Her long hair cradled her head like a fluffy golden pillow. He sat down next to her and leaned back on his hands.

"See those red flowers hanging over the water?" Sunflower had turned her head upstream and was pointing with her finger.

"I see them." Daniel could not recall ever seeing such a flower. But then, he never walked along creek banks looking for them. "They are pretty."

Sunflower looked at Daniel. "Do you see any other flowers?" she asked.

Daniel looked back at the red flowers she had called his attention to. And then he saw a nearby cluster of pale blue flowers. They were small and delicate. "There." He pointed. "And there." He pointed again, where a clump of green grass fell over a bank behind them and harbored the lavender petals of thin, flowering vines. Soon Daniel was pointing at places all around them.

Sunflower seemed to relish in the excitement of Daniel's discoveries. She raised up on her elbows and coaxed him on, until he had pointed out all of the little colorful secrets around them.

"You see, Daniel, there is color all around us. Even when you think it's not there, it is, waiting for you to discover it. I showed you the red flowers over there. But you found all of the others on your own. I knew you could see them. That is so important in this world. You must be able to see the colors. But not only the colors of flowers."

Daniel questioned Sunflower with his eyes.

"Look around me, Daniel." Sunflower raised up into a sitting position. "What do you see?"

"Butterflies." Daniel labored to say the word. "I see them." He had noticed them fluttering around since he and Sunflower had stepped out of the truck, and earlier that morning, when he saw her standing at the edge of the garden. He had even noticed when a butterfly followed her into Lucy's Café. But he had remained silent about it. "Why?" he finally asked. "Why do they follow you?"

Sunflower stood up and walked to the edge of the stream. For a minute, she looked upstream, away from Daniel. Then she bowed her head. Daniel thought she was praying. But when she turned around, she waved her hands out as if she were throwing seed, and scores of colorful winged skippers appeared in the tempered air around her. They lit upon her shoulders and arms. Sunflower looked at Daniel and then smiled and stepped into a streak of sunlight that had found its way through the thick foliage of the trees. She lifted her dress over her head and dropped it on the sand next to her. She raised her face to the sun and waved her hands out again. This time, more butterflies appeared, both large and small ones. A swirling frenzy of color surrounded the girl.

Daniel was amazed at what was happening before his eyes. He stood up, but remained silent.

Soon the butterflies began alighting on Sunflower's skin. Within a minute, they had settled upon her in such a way that her nakedness was hidden, and a magnificent and colorful winged gown graced the girl's body from her delicate shoulders down to the sand around her feet. A crown of fluttering beauty lent elegance to so radiant a sight that even the most captivating queen of nature would have been humbled in its presence.

After all the butterflies had settled on Sunflower's body, she opened her eyes and looked at Daniel with a peacefulness that mirrored the nature around them. "I am here for those willing to see the color in others, just as the little winged ones see the color in me."

Daniel looked at his hands. He could not begin to ask the questions churning in his head.

"It is not about the color of the skin, Daniel."

Sunflower raised her arms and shook her hands. The butterflies left her body in unison and blended into the surrounding forest.

Daniel picked up Sunflower's dress and handed it to her. She slipped it over her head and stepped out of the sunlight.

"It is about the color of one's spirit." Sunflower walked back over to her place in the sand and sat down. "Come and sit with me."

Daniel sat down.

"I know that you have seen the light that surrounds certain individuals you have known."

Daniel knew the light Sunflower was speaking of. He had seen it at times during his life. It was the brightest around his grandfather, but also in lesser brightness around his grandmother and other individuals he had known over the years. Benny Lester had it, and Lucy and Rita. Billy Meeks' light was strong just that day in the café. For years, Daniel had taken it for granted. He thought everyone could see what he saw. But one day when he was still a boy, he had asked his grandfather why the air was bright around him. Frank Taylor realized immediately that his grandson was able to see people beyond the physical, for he had learned through his own experiences that the light cast by the human spirit could radiate from its human bonds. At times, it served as a beacon to others. Frank had seen it when he was a boy, and as he grew older and wiser, he began to see not only the light around people, but also the myriad of colors that could be emitted by them. He told his grandson what he had learned in his life. And although he did not understand it all, Daniel had not forgotten.

"My papa said that the light was the language of the s...." Daniel could not get the word out.

"Spirit." Sunflower could feel Daniel's desire to express himself. "That is it, Daniel." She leaned toward him and continued. "Your papa was wise. He saw that light and the colors in other people. He knew that it was the language of the spirit reaching out. Some people can see it, and some can feel it. But you, Daniel, can do both."

"I can't see the color." Daniel seemed confused.

"You found the colors around you today. Most people would not have noticed. The world has sapped them of their ability to see the beauty around them, and worst of all, the beauty in each other. That is why I have come. I came through you. Your dreams mirrored your spirit. You saw me coming through a sunflower field, but I tell you that I have come through the beckoning of your spirit and the prayer you prayed from the core of your heart for the people of the world. That prayer was heard, Daniel, with all of the light and color of your spirit. It was heard."

Daniel could not stop the tears that welled in his eyes. Sunflower's fingers wiped them from his face. "I am only here for a while," she said. "Then I must begin my journey. But do not worry. I am not alone. Because of you and others like you, I am not alone."

Daniel swallowed and raked the sand around him with his fingers. There were so many questions he wanted to ask, but could not.

Sunflower knew his thoughts. "You asked me before why the butterflies come to me. They see my colors and believe that I am a flower garden."

Daniel smiled and looked at his friend. "What about...." He waved his hand as he had seen her do.

Sunflower laughed and lay back in the sand. "That is a gift, Daniel. Believe me."

Mary stood at the car door and watched Rosie settle into her seat behind the wheel.

"Don't you worry 'bout Daniel, Miz T," Rosie said as she shifted her weight in the seat. "He's goin' to be back home soon." She rolled down her window and pulled the car door shut.

"You know, Rosie, I'm not worried about him." Mary put her hands on the car door and leaned forward. "Maybe I should be, but for the first time I can recall, I'm not." She looked out toward the sunflower field. "Something is happening that I don't really understand. It's here in front of us, but it's bigger than we are. And I think Daniel has brought it here to Hopeful. That dream he had meant something. It was so strong that it went to his heart. And he has brought it here to us. He has somehow brought a dream to life."

Rosie reached up and gently patted Mary's hand. "We've always known he's a special one, Miz T. Maybe even those of us that's known him all along don't know just how special he really is."

Mary smiled and agreed. "God knows," she said softly.

Rosie started her car's engine. "That's for sure, Miz T. I'll see you in the mornin'. You rest tonight, knowin' it's all in God's hands. Everything. We don't have to know the reasons for it all."

"I'll see you tomorrow, Rosie." Mary stepped back from the car and watched as Rosie backed up and pulled away. She stood there for a while, until the sound of squeaking chains drew her attention to the cedar swing on the terrace above the garden. She looked in the direction of the sound and smiled when she saw clearly the straw hat that tilted just so on the head of a man she had come to trust as a friend. Mary was not surprised to see him again.

"Well, good evening, Mary." Isaac stood and raised his hand when the woman approached him. "Please sit with me." He offered her a place next to him on the swing.

"Thank you, Isaac." Mary sat down.

Isaac sat back down and placed his hat back on his head. "It is a beautiful evening." He looked up at the clear sky and then out at the field. "Daniel's sunflowers are just dazzling. Don't you agree?"

"Yes, they are." Mary could see the field of sunflowers more clearly than ever before. Other things were becoming clearer to her also. She looked at Isaac and felt that he was expecting her to say something. "This morning when I awoke, I saw the world around me in the blurred state I have become accustomed to. The flowers in my garden were beautiful with all their color, but there was no definition to their perfection. Only the knowledge that it was there. I saw Rosie when she arrived this morning, but the features of her big, kind face came only to my memory and not to my eyes. I looked in on Daniel as he slept and wished so that I could see the features of his handsome face. I sat in this swing that my husband placed here for me years ago and listened as the day began. It occurred to me that the majority of my life has passed, but I was not sad or even afraid. I heard the quiet cooing of a lone dove in the pear tree and although I could not see it, I could visualize it in my mind. My mind's reflections are clear, you know."

Isaac nodded his head. He allowed a comfortable silence between him and Mary to urge her contemplations to continue.

"A girl walked out of the sunflower field this morning, Isaac. I did not know her, but Daniel did. He said her name is Sunflower. I gave her a dress and food. She touched my shoulder. I told her she could stay here. I was tired, and while I slept, I dreamed that I followed her footsteps into the field, and there, in the shadows of the great flowers, I saw clearly the footprints of many others. I could feel their presence and hear their whisperings. I thought that I should be afraid, but I wasn't. They comforted me. When I awoke, I was aware that something miraculous had occurred." Mary closed her eyes and inhaled the warm, fragrant breeze of the August evening. Then she opened her eyes and turned her face toward Isaac. "Look at me, Isaac. Look deep into my eyes. Can you see that my sight has returned?"

Isaac looked even deeper into Mary's eyes. "Yes, Mary. I can see it."

"Then tell me what is happening here. Why did Daniel plant the sunflowers? Why has the girl come? Why can I see? You know the answers to my questions. I know you do."

Isaac stood up and walked to the edge of the terrace. He looked out at Daniel's beautiful flowers for a minute before he turned around and asked, "What do you think of the world, Mary?"

Mary shook her head. "That's a big question." She thought for a moment. "All my life it seemed that half the world was ending. Wars and plagues, earthquakes and floods. Raging storms. Broken-hearted people. Everything is so out of control. And yet, I've always felt that there was hope, even in the darkest times."

Isaac took off his hat and ran his fingers through his thick, white hair.

Mary thought he looked like a wise old philosopher, standing there in his crumpled linen suit. "Mary," he began, "if half the world is ending, then the other half is certainly beginning." He walked over and sat down beside her. "Listen to me," he urged. "There are changes coming to the earth that will seem like the end for mankind by those of little faith. It has already begun. Some of these changes have been subtle, and others will come with a force that will bring even the bravest man to his knees in fear. Lands will appear and disappear in the blink of an eye. Cold, dark shadows will cover the earth and interrupt the growing seasons. Plagues for which there will be no cures will be rampant. A cosmic upheaval will change the balance of the planet and render the powerful gadgets of men useless. Even the birds of the sky will be confused in these times when rivers flow backward and men are forced to become one with nature to survive. These things will happen, and as they do, all of the devastation, death, and suffering brought by men's foolish wars will be as nothing in comparison. The faithless will pray for death. The faithful will cling to hope. In these times, wars will cease as men draw unto one another for survival. This is the cleansing of the earth. The test for mankind." Isaac put his hat back on his head and adjusted the brim. He settled back against the cedar backrest. "You asked me why Daniel planted the sunflowers, Mary. The answer is that he was given a divine task, and he followed it without question. That is a testament to the pureness of his heart and the faith of his spirit. You ask why the girl has come, and I'll tell you this. God sends His messengers through the prayers of the faithful to come into the world and prepare the way. Sunflower is one of many. But the young man you raised as a son is one of only a few.

"Remember the book of Acts 2, Mary, and that

which was spoken by the prophet Joel: *And it shall come to pass in the last days, saith God, I will pour out of my Spirit upon all flesh: And your sons and your daughters shall prophesy, and your young men shall see visions, and your old men shall dream dreams: And on my servants and on my handmaidens I shall pour out in those days of my Spirit; and they shall prophesy: And I will show wonders in heaven above, and signs in the earth beneath; blood, and fire, and vapor of smoke: The sun shall be turned to darkness, and the moon into blood, before that great and notable day of the Lord comes: And it shall come to pass, that, whosoever shall call on the name of the Lord shall be saved.* You ask why your sight has returned, but now you must know that, in the presence of one who walks with the Lord, your own faith has healed you."

Mary's tears blurred her vision as she looked into the eyes of the man who had just revealed so much. There was one more question she wanted to ask but could not. She did not have to. The man beside her already knew.

"I am one who has walked this earth for many years. I have told the stories that were given to me, and I have answered the questions of true believers. It has been my duty to kneel with the soldiers on the battlefields and sit at the bedsides of those dying of illnesses. I am a protector of the children and the special ones who enrich the hearts and faith of all whom they touch." Isaac reached out and touched Mary's shoulder with his hand. "Mary, I was with your son during his last moments in this world. And I was with Daniel the day he was born, and on that morning your husband found him under the dogwood tree and brought him into your lives."

"You are his guardian angel," Mary whispered.

"I am." Isaac nodded his head. "And you must know that no matter what happens, you need not fear for him. I will always be nearby." Isaac smiled and handed Mary his handkerchief.

Mary dried her eyes and gave it back. "What now, Isaac?"

The man returned his handkerchief to his breast pocket, then pushed his hat back a little. "Well, let's walk along the flower garden path, and you can tell me how you and your husband planned your paradise here."

Mary smiled and stood. "It's a long story," she warned.

Isaac chuckled as he came to his feet. "Oh, that's all right, Mary. I have the time."

Forrest Meeks struggled with the bag of feed he was lifting into the bed of John Grayling's Chevy truck.

"Don't strain yourself, Forrest," warned John, who stood by with his hands on the feed cart. "I'd lend you a hand, but this back of mine has just about given out on me."

Forrest pushed the hundred-pound feed sack as far into the truck bed as he could, then looked at the three other bags and rubbed the back of his neck. "Don't worry about it, John. I reckon I can get them up here, one way or another."

John leaned down and gripped a corner of one of the bags. But he knew it was out of his league. "It's a shame Billy's not here today to show off a little muscle for us old fellas. Got him out on the road." Forrest reached down and started to grip the next sack when he realized that other hands had taken over. He raised up and admired the ease with which Daniel maneuvered the heavy sack into the bed of the truck. "Now, this is what we need, John. Look here."

Both men stepped back and watched Daniel lift and place the remaining feed sacks into the bed of the truck. He closed the gate and turned around. "Hello, Forrest." Daniel smiled and looked over at John. "Hi, John."

"Daniel, I believe you inherited the strength of your grandfather." John reached out and shook the young man's hand. "Frank was a powerful man."

"Who is your friend?" Forrest noticed the barefoot girl standing next to the young man. The warm afternoon breeze played with her tasseled hair and pressed her sundress against her body. Younger men would have sucked in their stomachs and puffed out their chests in their efforts to impress her, but Forrest and John were past such displays of virility. They simply admired her natural beauty, without lingering thoughts of what could never be.

"I am Sunflower," the girl spoke up as she stepped closer and reached out her hand.

Forrest shook her hand and stepped aside as John reached over the feed cart. "That's a right unusual name," he said, "and a pretty one, too."

Sunflower smiled and looked over at Daniel. "Daniel gave it to me," she admitted.

Forrest looked surprised. "So, it's not your real name?"

Sunflower saw the confusion on his face. She shrugged her shoulders. "Sure," was all she said.

"Where did you find this young lady, Daniel?" Forrest prided himself on his knowledge of the people in and around Hopeful.

"She came out of my sunflower field," Daniel answered innocently and without hesitation.

Both men looked at each other and laughed.

"Well, doggonit, Forrest." John slapped the handle on the feed cart with the palm of his hand. "Let's get back inside and settle up, and maybe I'll get me some of them sunflower seeds, too!"

Forrest chuckled. "Daniel, can you start working next week? Billy said he talked to you about it."

"I can," Daniel replied. "Is Billy back yet?"

"No, he's on the road to Vera this afternoon." Forrest turned toward the loading area of the store. "Daniel, if you could load those bales of straw onto the back of my truck over there, I'll tip you a little on your paycheck next week. Can you help me out on that?"

"I will," Daniel called back. He was already half-way across the lot.

"Thanks," Forrest said. "It was good to meet you." He smiled at Sunflower.

"So long." John was already in the shade of the loading area.

Sunflower smiled and waved her hand at the two men who disappeared into the shadows at the back of the store. She watched Daniel lift the straw bales onto Forrest's truck, paying little attention to the dirty black Bronco that pulled up behind her.

"Now that's more than I can take, brother." Bucky Scaggs turned off the Bronco's engine and leaned forward, biting the knuckles of his hands while gripping the steering wheel. "Look at that, Lonnie. Where'd he pick up somethin' like that?"

Lonnie sat straight up in his seat and chugged down the remainder of the beer in the bottle he had balanced on the seat between his legs. "I need a date tonight," he smirked. "How 'bout you, brother?" He laughed as he dropped the bottle in the truck's floorboard.

"Where we goin', Bucky?" Lonnie saw his brother push open his door.

Bucky stepped out of the truck. "I don't know." He laughed. "Revival, or somewhere. Does it matter?"

Lonnie looked around at the back of the feed and seed store. "Let's make it quick, Bucky," he warned.

Daniel watched the Scaggs brothers approach as he placed the last straw bale on Forrest Meeks' truck and walked between them and Sunflower. His eyes told her to beware.

Sunflower turned and faced the two ruffians.

"Hey, Taylor," Bucky called out, while his brother walked around behind Daniel. "Who's your friend, here?"

Daniel did not answer. He could feel his heart pounding as he recalled his last encounter with the two troublemakers.

Sunflower could sense the tension in the air. She could feel the lustful glare of Bucky's eyes exploring her body.

"He's a shy boy, Bucky," Lonnie teased. "He don't want to share his playmates with his old pals."

"My name is Sunflower." Sunflower moved closer to Daniel. She was not afraid, but cautious and protective. "And you are not Daniel's friends."

Bucky closed in. He noticed the girl was barefoot. A butterfly fluttered between her and Daniel and darted toward the older brother. Bucky swiped it out of the air in front of his face and crushed it between his fingers. "I hate these things," he said with disgust. He threw the lifeless creature to the pavement and mashed it with the toe of his boot. "I think Sunflower is a little bit of a hippy, brother. Look." He pointed. "She ain't got no shoes on her feet."

Lonnie was in a position where he could see the sunlight filtering through Sunflower's dress. He leaned on Daniel's shoulder. "Pardon me if I'm wrong, Taylor," he slurred, "but I'd swear she ain't wearin' anything under that little dress of hers. What ya think?"

Daniel jerked away from Lonnie. "Let's go." He moved closer to Sunflower.

Suddenly Bucky stepped between the two. "You

ain't goin' nowhere, idiot." There was a dangerous challenge in his voice.

Daniel's body tensed as he saw Bucky's fist shoot out from his side. The blow hit him below his belt. Immediately Daniel doubled over, grasping his abdomen and gasping for air.

Lonnie lurched forward then and kicked Daniel onto the gritty pavement. Daniel tried to get up, but Lonnie shoved him forward with his boot heel. "Stay down," he demanded.

Bucky pushed Sunflower's back against the truck bed and pressed his thick body against hers. The stench of his body was foul to her. His intent was clear. "Look here, Lonnie," Bucky boasted, his eyes studying the girl's lips. "This little hippy ain't got no fear of us." He placed his rough hands around her thin waist and began creeping up her ribs with his short, fat fingers, while peering lustfully down her dress. His voice became a low and savage growl. "Let's see what you ain't got on, you little…."

Lonnie was so enthralled with the audacity of his brother that he was not prepared for the blow that literally knocked him off his feet, shattering his jaw and breaking several of his teeth. His body had not hit the pavement before John Grayling knelt down and put his arm around Daniel's shoulder. John looked up and saw Forrest Meeks gripping Bucky's shirt collar in one hand while his fist was poised for a solid punch to the younger man's face.

Bucky's eyes were wide with fear. "I can't see!" he screamed. "I can't see!"

Forrest restrained himself and pushed Bucky away from him. "What do you mean you can't see?" He watched as Bucky rubbed at his eyes frantically and wandered aimlessly toward the loading area.

"My eyes!" Bucky cried. "They're burnin'! I can't see!"

"What's with him?" John asked as he and Sunflower helped Daniel to his feet. They walked him over to Forrest's truck, where Daniel sat on the open gate.

"Are you all right, Daniel?" Sunflower held Daniel's face in her hands.

Daniel nodded his head. "I'm okay." He looked at John. "Thank you," he said.

John looked behind him at Lonnie Scaggs, who was now in a sitting position, holding his jaw in both hands and spitting blood and teeth onto the crotch of his jeans. John looked back at Daniel and put his hand on the young man's shoulder. "It's best he took a lick from me instead of you, Daniel. I've seen how strong you are." John winked.

"Sunflower." Forrest approached the back of the truck. "Are you okay?" He looked over at Lonnie and then out at the loading lot where Bucky was on his knees, sobbing. "I'm so sorry about this. These two have been causing trouble ever since they came to Hopeful. They were drunk in my store last week, and I kicked them out. I'm sorry this happened."

"I am fine, Forrest." Sunflower touched Daniel's forehead tenderly with her hand. She stood and looked out at Bucky.

"We should call the sheriff, Forrest." John put his hands in his pockets and leaned against the truck's back fender.

"No." Sunflower walked out to where Bucky was crawling on his hands and knees.

"Better be careful," John warned. He calmly packed the bowl of his pipe with tobacco and glanced back at Lonnie. "They're mean as snakes."

Bucky was down on his knees, rubbing his eyes when he felt Sunflower's presence. "You blinded me." His face was wet and dirty. His eyes, red and swollen.

"Your sin blinded you." Sunflower knelt beside the stricken man. She could sense his fear, the darkness in his heart. "Listen to me and heed what I say."

Bucky faced the girl in silent agony. He could feel his heartbeat in his throat.

"For all of your life you have scorned, belittled, and harmed all things that are beautiful. There has been no purpose in the wicked things you have done. No reasoning, and no direction in your life. Your heart is in a black hole of despair, where fear and anger fuel your every decision. But I tell you there is a ladder of light that will lead you out of your darkness. Open your heart and your mind to the God of all, and you will see that light come down."

Bucky closed his swollen eyes and lowered his head. His tears fell like raindrops onto the pavement. "Can God save me?" Bucky's voice was a raspy whisper.

"He will forgive you and allow you to save yourself," Sunflower answered. "Nothing is beyond His power, and all things are possible through faith in Him."

"I'm afraid." Bucky lifted his face to Sunflower. He could not open his eyes.

The girl placed her hand on his shoulder. "Come out of the blackness of your despair. Climb the ladder of light and feel the hand of God."

Bucky listened to the words of the girl he had tried to defile and his shame was such that he gripped his chest with his hands. His heart fluttered, and speckles of light appeared behind his eyelids. His head swam for a moment, and he felt as if he would fall over, except for the support of Sunflower's hand on his shoulder. When he opened his eyes, he could see the face of the girl. But it was in the wells of her dark eyes that he perceived the one thing he desired most of her. "You forgive me." Emotion choked his whisper. He tried to repeat his words, but could not.

Sunflower's voice was gentle. "Yes. I forgive you." She stood and offered her hand. "Now, go to your brother. He needs you."

Bucky took Sunflower's hand and rose to his feet. He wiped his eyes and blinked them repeatedly. "I don't know what to say."

"Yes, you do." Sunflower looked back at the men standing at the rear of Forrest's truck. Lonnie was standing alone.

"Go and say it to your brother, and then to everyone who will listen. Tell them that a change has begun in this world, and that a spiritual reckoning is coming. Tell them to seek the light of God."

Bucky Scaggs apologized to Daniel for the cruelty he and his brother had brought upon him. He apologized to Forrest for the drunken disrespect they had displayed in his store.

After the Scaggs brothers had left, Forrest and John said their goodbyes to Daniel and Sunflower. For a while, the two older men sat quietly on the open gate of Forrest's truck. John puffed on his pipe, while Forrest seemed content with the peace that surrounded them.

"Well, I guess we'll be thinking about all this for a while," Forrest said as he watched a pigeon fly down into the loading area, where spilled seed lay scattered.

"Yep. I reckon we will," John agreed.

Forrest looked over at John. A smile creased his lips. "You know, for an old codger with a bad back, you sure gave that fella a wallop."

John finished his pipe and began cleaning its bowl with the blade of his pocket knife. "You know, Forrest, the funny thing is, my back don't hurt no more."

For some reason, Forrest was not surprised.

Daniel looked at his watch. It was 5:15 PM. He turned his truck off of Main Street and headed up Second Avenue.

Sunflower was enjoying looking at the houses and the vehicles parked along the street. "There are no children playing. There are no people." She did not seem surprised.

"They're inside, watching TV, I guess." Daniel had never thought about the fact that folks were spending their time indoors.

Sunflower was quiet for a minute. "They should be outside," she finally said.

Daniel shrugged his shoulders. "Dangerous to let the children play outside. They have video games in the house."

Sunflower shook her head. "That is so sad."

"There's folks over at the Corner Store. Look." Daniel pointed up the street.

Sunflower leaned forward in her seat, her hands on the dashboard. "Stop. I want to see them."

Daniel pulled the truck into the store's parking lot and sat looking at a small crowd of people standing at the front of the store. He opened his door and stepped out. A few people in the crowd looked back at him and either put up their hands or shook their heads.

Benny Lester backed away from where he was standing and approached Daniel's truck.

"Hi, Benny." Daniel stood beside his truck. Sunflower had scooted across the seat behind the steering wheel.

"We got us a situation over there at the steps." Benny seemed nervous.

"What is it?" Sunflower stepped down from the truck and stood beside Daniel.

Benny looked toward the store and shook his head. "Tom and Hilda's three-year-old granddaughter was playing around the steps there and has cornered a copperhead. That thing is coiled up and ready to strike the girl. They're trying to talk her into staying still, hoping the snake will get tired and go away. Tom has a shovel ready to kill it, but he's afraid any movement will cause it to bite the girl."

Benny shook his head. "I'm not so sure the little girl is not going to move in a minute. This standoff has been going on for over ten minutes now, and you know how a child is."

Sunflower had already started toward the crowd when Benny said, "It'd be best not to go over there." He looked at Daniel.

"Her name is Sunflower." Daniel stepped around Benny and followed the girl.

"Stay back!" Tom Yeatts warned when he saw Sunflower emerge from the crowd of people who were standing in a semi-circle behind the little girl. "Hold still, Betsy," he urged his granddaughter. "Don't move, honey."

Sunflower could feel the intensity of Tom's fear. His aura had spread out into the crowd. Everyone was anxious. But the little girl was not afraid.

"The snake will not strike the child," Sunflower said calmly.

"Who the hell are you?" Tom was irritated.

"Her name is Sunflower, Tom." Benny was now standing behind Sunflower and next to Daniel. "She's with Daniel."

Tom looked at Daniel, then back at Sunflower. "How do you know?" he asked.

"Your fear has put a threat of danger in the air. Everyone feels it—even the snake." Sunflower's self-assurance was evident. "Betsy has no fear and has shown no aggression. But the snake is confused. The last thing it wants to do is waste its venom on a non-threatening entity." Sunflower moved slowly toward the little girl. "Let me talk to her."

"What can I do?" Tom was willing to do anything to save his granddaughter from a painful and life-threatening experience.

Sunflower looked at the man standing on the porch a few steps above the scene. In his hand was the handle of a raised garden shovel.

"Back away, slowly, sir." Sunflower's voice was one of quiet authority. "Everyone must back away from here, slowly. Your fear has permeated this place."

Within a minute, only Sunflower stood close to the little girl. Everyone else watched from a distance.

"I hope she knows what she's doing," Hilda said nervously. "Oh, God. That snake could bite Betsy in the face."

"Don't worry." Daniel patted Hilda on the shoulder. "She's going to be all right."

Hilda looked at Daniel and then over at Benny Lester. The man tightened his lips and shrugged.

Sunflower could not see the little girl's face from where she stood, but she knew the nature of a young child. Cautiously, she knelt behind the girl. "Do not move until I tell you to, Betsy. You will feel my hand touch your shoulder and see my other hand reaching out beside you. My name is Sunflower, and I will not cause harm to you. The snake does not wish to strike you, but it is confused."

Betsy was holding a red rubber ball in her left hand. Her right hand was resting on her raised knee. The touch of Sunflower's hand on her shoulder comforted her.

"Do not be afraid, Betsy," Sunflower said as she reached her right hand out in front and away from the girl. "Now, rise up slowly, step back and around me." Sunflower could see that the snake's attention was now drawn to her outstretched hand, which was closer than the child. Slowly, she urged the girl up and back until she alone was in reach of the snake's strike. "Go now," she whispered.

As soon as the child had moved away from it, the snake uncoiled and slithered to the end of the concrete step and into the guillotine of the sharp edge of Tom Yeatt's shovel.

Hilda ran to her grandchild and smothered her with hugs.

"Thank you," Tom said as he scooped up the head of the copperhead and began walking toward the back of the store.

"That was close." Benny rubbed the back of his neck. "She's a real snake charmer, Daniel. Where did she come from?"

"My sunflower field." Daniel followed Hilda into the store and came out with two cold sodas. He handed one to Sunflower, who was sitting on the porch step with Betsy and two other children. Within a half-hour's time, several other children had joined them. Soon there were more children from the community on the porch steps of the corner store than Tom and Hilda Yeatts had seen in a long time. They listened to Sunflower's stories and songs and chased butterflies in the grass beyond the parking lot, while their parents watched from inside the store and talked amongst themselves.

Sheriff Bob Grills hung up the telephone and pushed back from his desk. He drummed the edge of the hardwood desktop with his index fingers for a minute, lost in thought.

"Oden." He leaned forward in his chair and called toward his office door. "Oden. Are you out there?" The sheriff heard the shuffle of papers and then the sound of his deputy pushing back his chair.

A few footsteps later, Oden Holman stood at the office door. "What's up, sir?"

"Come in, Oden." Sheriff Grills leaned back in his chair and locked his hands around the back of his head. "I just got a call from Jenny Altice over at the medical clinic, and she said the Scaggs brothers were by there a little while ago."

"Oh?" Oden stepped into the office, his thumbs locked over his gun belt.

"Yeah. Jenny says the younger brother, Lonnie, was all busted up with a broken jaw and some teeth gone. She said neither Lonnie or his brother, Bucky, was offering much reason for it."

Oden knew the Scaggs brothers. It seemed he was always questioning them about some trouble they were involved in. "You think they might have just scrapped it out between themselves? They're about as mean as junkyard dogs. Could've gotten liquored up."

Sheriff Grills raised his eyebrows. "I don't know. Maybe. But you might just check it out. I don't want to find that they've left someone lying in a ditch somewhere." The sheriff un-cupped his hands and stood up. He walked around the corner of his desk and sat on its edge. "You know anything about a local girl named Sunflower?"

"Sunflower?" Oden had never heard the name. "No, sir, can't say that I do."

"Well, Jenny says Bucky was spouting off some religious mumbo jumbo and mentioned this girl a couple of times. That's a strange coincidence, because Sammy Goode told my wife that a girl named Sunflower charmed a copperhead this afternoon over at the corner store. Said she was riding with Mary Taylor's grandson, Daniel. Sammy saw the whole thing." The sheriff stood and walked back around to his chair. "You might check that out, too. If this Sunflower girl can beat the fool out of Lonnie Scaggs and charm a snake at the same time, I'd like to deputize her."

Oden chuckled. "I'll check it out, sir." He turned around and exited the office. "Sunflower," Oden repeated the name. *If she's connected in any way to the Taylor family, Mama will know*, he thought. *I'll talk with her tonight.*

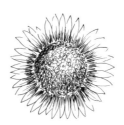

"I looked through the clothing I was packing up for the Goodwill and found another sundress and a few other things you might like, Sunflower." Mary Taylor handed the last supper plate to the girl as she spoke. "We're going to have to get you some undergarments tomorrow."

"Thank you. You are so kind to me, Mary." Sunflower dried the plate according to Mary's instructions and put it with the others in the open cabinet over the counter.

"Let's go out on the patio." Mary walked to the door. "It's such a clear evening. I'll bet the stars are already out." She peered up and drew a long breath. "I thought they'd be magnificent. Just look."

Sunflower took in the twinkling display and agreed. She sat down in a chair next to Mary. "I had an interesting time with Daniel today."

"Oh? Did he show you our little town?"

"Yes, he did, and we even walked in the creek."

Mary studied Sunflower's face in the light that filtered over from the lamppost at the edge of the flower garden. "I think Daniel knew you would come."

"Yes, Mary, he did. He named me, you know. I like my name."

"What is your real name?" Mary felt at ease with Sunflower and did not think she would mind her question.

"I have had many names, Mary. It is the way for the messengers."

"So you've been here before?"

"I have been here many times. This world is vast, and the generations pass quickly. There are so many who must hear."

"Hear what?" Mary wanted to hear again what she already knew from her talk with Isaac.

"The message is the truth, Mary. You can find it in a dream, or a vision, or in the eyes of a newborn baby. You can feel it in the force of nature, read it in the words of the prophets. The realization of the truth will erase one's fear of death, for He has already taken that burden. Believe me, Mary, when I tell you that the kingdom of God is only a breath away."

Mary felt a pang of guilt. "I told Daniel that to know the truth, he must sleep on a sunflower. He wanted to know the truth of his dream. It is an old-wives'-tale. A legend. I didn't really think he would do it."

Sunflower smiled. "Daniel is a pure heart. He is special. That is why he was brought to you and your husband. The caretakers of the special ones are chosen carefully, for they must be wise in their guidance for the time they are in charge. The pure hearts must not be led astray. Do not feel guilt in what you told him, Mary. You have been wise. And you have elevated the beauty and relevance of a sunflower to a level befitting its radiance.

"Daniel knew I would come. It was his purpose to bring me here. But it is not finished. Instinctively, he knew that only the children and the special ones were to plant the seeds of the field. And, likewise, they shall sleep with their heads upon the flower, to bring his dream to its fruition."

Mary reached out and touched Sunflower's hand. "I am humbled by the things you have told me."

Sunflower squeezed Mary's hand. "And I am thankful for the kindness you have shown me."

Rosie Holman put her bags down on the kitchen counter. "Miz T, I brought those undergarments you asked for. I think they'll fit. She ain't nothing but a little thing. I'll lay them out on your bed, and you can show them to our little flower child."

Mary finished her cup of coffee and walked over to the counter. She looked at the garments. "Very nice. She'll like these."

Rosie noticed the door to Daniel's room was open. "Where's Daniel?" she asked.

"He was up early this morning. I couldn't get him to eat any breakfast. All he wanted was a glass of juice. He met Sunflower out at the cedar swing, and they went out to the field together." Mary stood at the kitchen sink and looked out the window. "She's here for a reason, Rosie." Mary turned and looked at the woman. "You know, you and I have always said that there is a reason for everything."

Rosie wiped the countertop with a dry dish towel. She folded it neatly and placed it over her shoulder. "I know it, Miz T. And I know that young man you raised out there is a part of that reason."

"Yes, he is," Mary agreed. "All his life, he has struggled to find his place in this world. From the time he could walk, he wanted to be like everyone else. But he couldn't. There was no way he could keep up with the children his age. They all left him behind. Even the ones who knew him best just naturally went on with their lives. But Daniel could not do that. He has stayed here and has still somehow touched so many people. Children love him, and old people are lifted by his hugs and his smile."

"Yes, they are." Rosie knew the truth in everything Mary said about Daniel. She knew the joy of his presence.

"I was thinking this morning, Rosie, of how small Daniel's world must seem to him. And it made me sad, until I thought about all of those people whose lives he has touched, just by showing he cares for them.

Daniel's world is really not so small after all."

"I think you've said it right, Miz T." Rosie smiled. "That young man's world is bigger than we know."

"Where are you going to go?" Daniel threw a rock into a fence row covered with honeysuckle. He watched the blond girl walking barefoot along the edge of the flower field.

Sunflower stopped and turned around. She walked back to Daniel and stood, looking up at him. The morning sun bronzed his tan face. His brown eyes peered into hers with a depth of wisdom that would humble a poet. She touched his face with her hand. "You know I must go out into the world, Daniel," she answered. "That is why I have come."

Daniel looked down for a moment at his friend's bare feet. "You will have to wear shoes, Sunflower."

Sunflower smiled back at him. "I will wear shoes," she promised.

"I could go with you." Daniel was serious.

Sunflower could see sincerity in the colors of his aura. "You could," she began, "but then the people of Hopeful would not have you to inspire them and bring hope to their hearts in the days that are to come. A town needs a man such as you, Daniel. One who has risen above the challenges of his life, and who is not afraid of the things he cannot explain. The people around you always need to see the wisdom and fearlessness in the one who will follow his heart."

Daniel noticed the butterflies that had begun to collect around the girl. A yellow and black swallowtail lit upon her raised finger. She offered it to him, and he was surprised when the winged creature climbed into the palm of his hand. "You won't be alone?" Daniel struggled with his words but not their meaning.

Sunflower understood his concern, for the world beyond the limits of his travel seemed dark and dangerous to him. "I will never be alone, Daniel," she responded confidently, "and neither will you."

Daniel looked at the butterfly in his hand, then back at the girl. "When will you leave?" he asked.

"When the others have come." Sunflower shooed the butterfly from Daniel's palm. She took his hand in hers and urged him to walk beside her into the shadows of the great, towering flowers. The warm August breeze swept over the field as the two disappeared beneath the shimmering mirror of the sun.

Later that day, Billy Meeks held the line of his fishing reel taut as he followed the bubbled streaks in the pond's smooth surface with excited eyes. "I've got one!" he shouted to Daniel, who stood nearby. "He's gliding along the bottom. Bound to be one of those catfish your granddaddy put in here a few years ago."

Daniel pulled in his bare hook and laid his rod against a birch sapling. He walked over and stood with his hands on his hips. "Papa caught them sometimes," he said. "He let them tire out on their own."

"You ever catch one, Daniel?" Billy's voice was a pitch higher than usual.

"No." Daniel shook his head.

"You ever eat one?" Billy reeled the line in a little bit at a time. "I'll bet these are some good eatin' cats."

Daniel shook his hear vigorously. "No," he answered. "I don't eat fish."

"Why not?" asked Billy in a surprised tone.

"Too fishy." Daniel shrugged.

"Shoot, Daniel," Billy replied, "if they're fixed up right, they don't taste like fish at all."

"What do they taste like?" Daniel had never been fond of fish, no matter how his grandmother prepared them, and would only occasionally eat store-bought fish sticks smothered in catsup. He had enjoyed fishing with his grandfather, but only for sport. He would never consider eating a catch of fish and would always give them to Rosie Holman, whose husband, Henry, was fond of pond fish.

"They taste like a cat," Billy teased.

Daniel turned from his friend in mock disgust. "No way!" he laughed.

Billy pulled the heavy catfish onto the grassy bank. He reached down and patted the white belly of the fish with his hand. "The fillets from this fish will feed me, Rita, and your grandma for supper tonight." He looked up at Daniel and grinned. "You reckon Rosie will fix it up for us?"

Daniel leaned over and looked at the prostrate catfish. "She will, if you catch one for Henry."

Billy pulled the hook from the lip of the fish with a pair of pliers from his tackle box. He grasped the fish behind the sharp spines that grew out from its sides and sank it gently into a water-filled bucket. "I can do that," he said, while readjusting the ragged piece of liver on the hook.

Daniel watched Billy cast the line into the pond. "Papa skinned them over there." He pointed to a cedar tree at the edge of the pond, shaded by the nearby forest. "Rosie won't clean them."

Billy felt the tug of another catfish and brought the tip of his rod up quick. "Got it," he said. He looked over at the board nailed to the cedar tree. "I'll clean 'em." He looked behind him. "Where did the girls go?" He wanted Rita to watch him bring in another fish.

Daniel pointed up the hill at a shady grove of oak trees. "Up there," he answered. "She can see you."

Billy turned and spied the two girls. He waved at them, then got back to his task.

Daniel lumbered to a grassy knoll and lay down on

his back with his hands under his head. A long, grey cloud took away the heat from the sun, and he closed his eyes and waited for Billy to interrupt his rest.

It was cooler up the little hollow from the pond under the sprawling oak trees. Rita and Sunflower sat at the base of one of the trees on a bale of straw Daniel had placed there for them. He had insisted on bringing it there so they could sit in comfort while he and Billy fished.

"Guess what we're gonna have for supper tonight," Sunflower teased.

"Billy loves to fish." Rita bent the stem of straw in her fingers while she watched Billy reel in his catch.

"He loves you, Rita." The tone of Sunflower's voice brought comfort to Rita. Her words reinforced what the girl already knew.

Rita felt a closeness with Sunflower. If Lucy Wenby was her adopted mother, then surely Sunflower was her instant best friend. Rita's heart opened. "I know he loves me. He told me so." Rita's voice began to break, and she stopped for a moment before continuing. "He said he wants to marry me and be a father to my child. He said no child should be born without a father." Rita set the stem of straw on her knee and straightened it with her forefinger. "I'm afraid I bring along a lot of baggage, Sunflower. I mean, look at me. Abused by my own parents, and then left this way by a boy who promised me the world and gave me…." Rita looked down and rested her hand on her stomach.

"A chance at a new life," Sunflower finished her sentence for her.

Rita closed her eyes and shook her head.

Sunflower continued. "Life is a gift with no guarantees, Rita. It is a series of choices you make, and then your reactions to the consequences of those choices. But you must understand that you will be affected by the choices of others, too. That is why you are here. Your reaction to the choices made toward you was to go as far away as your money could take you. That choice has brought you to Hopeful. This is where it begins. Look at who found you."

"Daniel." Rita smiled.

"Yes, Daniel. A true and caring soul, who brought you into the arms of one who has accepted you as if you were her own daughter."

"Lucy," Rita whispered, as tears welled in her eyes.

"Yes. And I am sure that it is as clear to her as it is to those of us around you that you are in love with Billy."

"But…." Rita was crying.

Sunflower raised her eyebrows. "Don't let the fears of another life spoil your chance for a new one. Believe me when I tell you that life is much too short for a mistake such as that." Sunflower looked down the hill. "That young man, pulling the fish out of the water, loves you with all of his heart, and is willing to accept you as you are. That is a gift in itself. If you love him, you must trust him."

Rita wiped the tears from her eyes. "It is my choice to make."

"No one else's," Sunflower agreed. "Choose wisely."

Oden Holman smelled the seasoning his mother had sprinkled over the generous portion of catfish fillet that lay on his plate. It was surrounded by fresh lima beans, mashed potatoes and gravy and thin-buttered cornbread. "Mama, where in the world did you find such a fish?" he asked while eyeing the large portion his father was about to slice into.

Rosie sat down at the supper table and poured herself a glass of milk. "Billy Meeks caught it this afternoon over at the Taylor's pond."

"You mean the one below the old corn field?" Oden followed his question with a bite of fish.

"That's the one." Rosie worked the gravy into her potatoes and looked over at her husband.

"Henry, you need some more lima beans?" She offered him the steaming bowl.

Henry waved it off. "Not right now, honey. Soon as I eat some of this catfish, I'll have room on the plate for it."

"Um, this is good." Oden reached over and sliced a thin pat of butter off the end of the butter stick and spread it over his cornbread. "Mama, you know anything 'bout a girl named Sunflower? Sheriff Grills says she's a friend of Daniel's."

Henry washed his food down with a gulp of water.

"That's the girl you was tellin' me 'bout last night, ain't it, honey?"

Rosie straightened her napkin in her lap. "Why, yes, she's a friend of the Taylors, and I was telling you about her last night, Henry." Rosie stuck the tip of her fork into a chunk of fish and put it in her mouth.

"Well?" Oden waited for his mother to continue.

"Well, what?" Rosie drank her milk and dipped a large lima bean into her mashed potatoes and gravy. She started to put it to her lips.

"The sheriff wants to know about her." Oden kept eating.

Rosie felt annoyed that Sheriff Grills would be interested at all in a girl that just came to town. She put her fork down. "Like I said, she's a friend of the Taylor family, who came in yesterday. She's blonde, with brown eyes, pretty as a flower, and about as big as a minute." Rosie moved her cornbread on her plate. "What has got Bob Grills so interested in that child, tell me?"

Oden could sense his mother's irritation. "Don't get all bothered about it, Mama. It's just that Sammy Goode was over at the corner store yesterday and said that Tom and Hilda Yeatts' little granddaughter got cornered on the steps by a copperhead and was about to get bit, when this girl shows up with Daniel and charms it away. Then the Scaggs brothers show up at the clinic, and one of them has been beaten up pretty bad. They wouldn't tell who did it, but did mention the girl's name. Just curious, I guess. The sheriff just likes to know who's in town."

Rosie chuckled. "Well, I guess if he was that finicky 'bout who's in town, he would've been a little more observin' of those Scaggs brothers, wouldn't he?"

"Mama." Oden put up his hands in resignation.

But his mother continued. "You tell the good sheriff that I ain't seen nothin' of no snake charmer 'round the Taylor's place, and that no girl has beat up no Scaggs boy, although it's 'bout time somebody around here did."

"Well, Mama, that's fine. It's not as if he's investigatin' her."

"Oh?" Rosie looked over at her husband.

Henry avoided eye contact with her and seemed seriously devoted to his supper.

"Do you know where she's from?" Oden knew it would be his last question concerning the girl.

"Yes, as a matter of fact, I do, Son." Rosie straightened herself in her chair. "You tell the sheriff that she just walked right out of that big sunflower field of Daniel's, naked as a jaybird, and they named her on the spot." She looked over at Henry and tipped her head. The man smiled nervously and stuffed a break of cornbread in his mouth.

Oden rolled his eyes and looked at his mother until her expression told him to change the subject. He looked down at his plate and scraped up a fork-full of catfish. "This is about the best-tastin' fish I've ever had, Mama," he said respectfully.

Rosie smiled. "That's good, Son. I have a big ol' piece of cherry pie for you and your daddy, too."

Henry Holman looked up at his wife and grinned.

"There." Mary Taylor pinned a fresh-cut flower in a wave of Sunflower's hair near her temple. She pushed the girl's golden locks back over her shoulders and stood back to take it all in. "You look absolutely stunning." The pale blue sundress she had worn in her younger days fit Sunflower perfectly. Mary was pleased. The dress had been one her husband often complimented her on.

"Do the garments Rosie brought you fit all right?"

Sunflower pulled at the elastic just below her hips with her fingers. "I'll get used to them, Mary."

Mary smiled. She thought about adding some makeup to Sunflower's face, but then thought better of it. There was little that could improve her complexion. "You will like our church." Mary turned and looked at her own face in the mirror. "Today's a special day for the young people." She added a touch of lipstick to her thin lips and pressed them together.

Sunflower watched the woman with interest. "Daniel says many children will be there." The girl looked at her lips in the mirror and pressed them together, mimicking Mary.

"Yes, and I think he knows them all." Mary put the lid on her lipstick tube and dropped it in her purse. "We're ready," she announced.

Sunflower followed Mary out of the bedroom and through the house, into the kitchen. Daniel was waiting at the patio door.

His eyes widened when he saw Sunflower. "You look pretty." His compliment came with a smile.

"Thank you, Daniel." Sunflower approached him and touched his tie. "Butterflies," she said, while studying the colorful images painted on the material. "I like it."

Daniel was proud of the butterfly tie he had purchased at a local craft festival. He had never worn it, but felt that today was the opportune time for its debut. He looked down at the tie and rubbed his fingers along its length, as if to smooth it out. "I like it, too," he said.

"Are we ready to go?" Mary headed for the door.

Sunflower looked at Daniel with questioning eyes. He winked at her.

"Yes, Mary," the girl answered. "We are ready."

"What a glorious morning." Mary walked along the pathway toward the car. "Goodness, look at all the butterflies out this morning." Mary had never seen so many of the little winged creatures fluttering throughout her garden. "Did you call them in, Sunflower?" she asked.

"They just know to come." Sunflower laughed when a little snout butterfly with warm, brown wings lit upon the ridge of Daniel's nose.

Daniel crossed his eyes to look at the tiny passenger. He opened the car door for his grandmother, and the butterfly skipped away. Daniel closed the door and turned to Sunflower. "Isaac helped me," he said. "We put them in sacks. They're in the trunk of the car."

Sunflower looked across the flower garden toward the terrace, where the old man was sitting in the cedar swing.

Isaac Heartwell turned his face to the girl, smiled and tipped the brim of his straw hat.

Sunflower nodded her head and stepped into the car. As they drove away, a lone dove cooed from a shaded branch in the pear tree at the edge of the yard. Isaac smiled at the sound and began to swing back and forth.

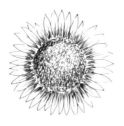

Youth Sunday was a special time for the young people in the town of Hopeful. It was the one day set aside during the year when churches of all denominations came together to worship as one. The children sat together, mindless of the rituals, traditions, and politics of their parents' chosen church associations. This day was founded by a young minister who served a local church years before, hoping that the importance of a spiritual life would enter into the hearts and minds of the young. That minister had convinced the church-going community that it was crucial for the children to come together in one accord, as the world they were experiencing was but a shadow of what the generations before them had known.

The young Reverend Milan Reno had felt that a desecration of humanity was eroding the human spirit to the point where people were becoming islands unto themselves, afraid to open their hearts to each other. He told his congregation and others that this spiritual affliction was worldwide and more devastating than any plague the news media could trump. Reverend Reno said that the wise and the just of the world had become quiet and complacent, while the foolish and unjust wielded their powers. He sensed the loss of morality and felt in his heart that the fate of man was at hand. Although secure in his own salvation, the young reverend feared for the children who were growing up in a society which, day-by-day, seemed bent on separating itself from the very foundation of its existence. It was that fear that awoke him in the middle of the night and brought heartfelt prayers to his lips. Perhaps it was from that fear that he dreamed of a church filled with children—a glorious church, light with color and hearts strong with faith. A sanctuary where doubtless and willing souls came together as one. It was a very real dream, and one Milan Reno was not afraid to bring to fruition. It became part of his calling in life. So much so that in all the places he went to preach the word of God, he also took his dream.

Sunflower stood at the edge of the church parking lot and stared at the white letters arranged beneath the glass of the brick-framed billboard. A bed of flowers of mixed varieties grew at the base of the structure. She heard an elderly woman comment on the beauty of the flowers as the woman shuffled by the billboard on her way across the church lawn. The steeple bell was ringing as Sunflower stepped into the grass of the church yard. Immediately, she reached down and pulled off her shoes. The cool, soft grass felt good between her toes.

Mary Taylor looked back at Sunflower and then at Daniel. Her grandson shrugged his shoulders. The girl looked at them both and smiled. "Look at all the children, Mary," she commented.

Mary noticed that several of the youngsters had seen Sunflower remove her shoes and were duplicating her expression of freedom. One or two of the parents threw suspicious glances toward Sunflower.

A little girl, followed by her grandmother, made her way through the crowd of people. Hilda Yeatts greeted Mary, while Betsy walked straight to Sunflower and raised up her hands. Sunflower immediately recognized the little girl and picked her up. "Hello, Betsy," she said. "I'm so glad to see you again."

"Hi, Sunflower." Betsy touched the flower Mary had pinned in Sunflower's hair. "I like the flower in your hair."

Sunflower reached around back of the child's head and brought back a colorful surprise. "And I like the little crescent butterfly you wear in your hair." The small butterfly was perched calmly on Sunflower's index finger.

Betsy giggled and tried to touch the wing of the butterfly, but it flew up in the air, over her head. "I didn't know I had a butterfly in my hair." Betsy giggled again.

Sunflower touched the girl on the nose. "It thought you were a little flower."

Betsy laughed and hugged her new friend.

"Thank you for what you did yesterday." Hilda reached out and Sunflower put Betsy in her arms. "I was so frightened for her."

Sunflower smiled. "She is lovely."

"What happened?" Mary was perplexed. She looked at Daniel, and then at Hilda.

"They didn't tell you about the snake on the steps of the store, and how Sunflower charmed it away from harming our little girl?" Hilda put Betsy down and held her hand.

Mary looked at Daniel inquisitively. "No, they didn't tell me about that."

"Daniel!" a child called from out in the yard. Daniel recognized the voice and turned.

Sunflower followed him through the crowd.

"She is really something, Mary." Hilda walked beside Mary into the church.

"Yes, she is," Mary agreed. "She really something."

By the time the church door was closed, there was a capacity crowd in the sanctuary. The large balcony was occupied by the adults. The pews were filled, and some had to sit in chairs along the side walls of the sanctuary, beneath the beautiful stained-glass windows.

Mary looked for Daniel and Sunflower but could not locate them. She was still amazed at the return of her eyesight and was happy that even the children sitting in the choir seats were recognizable to her. She saw Reverend Milan Reno sitting in a chair behind the pulpit. Several youth-ministers from area churches were in chairs near him. They would help guide the service along. However, the young people would share stories of witness and sing moving songs that would carry the theme of the gathering. Mary could see Benny Lester sitting near the front of the church with several of the special ones who were able to come. Daniel would often sit with them, but she did not see him among them.

Just then, Rita Sedgeway tapped Mary on the shoulder. Mary turned around in her seat and saw Rita sitting beside Billy Meeks. "Good morning," Mary said. "I didn't even notice you behind me this morning. Isn't it wonderful to see this big church so full of people?"

"Good morning, Mimi." Rita had a certain radiance about her. Mary could see she was happy.

"How are you, dear?" Mary reached back and grasped the girl's hand.

Rita smiled. "I'm fine, Mimi." She looked at Billy. "I'm really fine." Then she leaned forward slightly and spoke softly. "Billy asked me to marry him, and I said yes."

"That's wonderful, dear!" She smiled at Billy. "I'm so happy for you both. Now everything is going to be just fine. I'll say a prayer for you."

Rita smiled and sat back in her seat. "Thank you, Mimi."

"Did you see Daniel?" Mary asked.

"Yes," Billy answered. "He and Sunflower were outside talking to some children in the yard a little while ago. I didn't see them come in."

Mary nodded her head and turned back around in her seat.

The service ran long that morning, with all the stories and songs. The youth ministers read scriptures and urged the young people to be wise and patient and to have faith in the Lord.

Mary Taylor was touched by the service and thought it was the way it should be. But when Milan Reno stood up and addressed the congregation, something occurred that Mary would have never expected.

"Many years ago," the old minister began, "I dreamed of a day when all children would come together in the name of the Lord. I saw them doing just as you have done today, singing songs and telling your stories. That dream was so overwhelming to me then that I could not put it out of my mind. I followed it, went with it, and made it come true." Reverend Reno paused and looked out over the gathering of people. "It warms my heart to see you all here today in one accord. It is good that I have seen this in other communities, also, for these are uncertain times, when one's faith is tested daily, and the light of hope can dim beneath despairing clouds." The minister touched the Bible on the stand in front of him. "I often wonder if my dream was prophetic. A truth. One that I should know. I am glad I did not let it go. For somehow, I feel that I was meant to act upon it. You see, I believe that if a vision comes from one unselfish prayer, then you must follow it and know its truth.

"Prayers from the heart will be answered. And when those answers come, do not ignore them."

Milan Reno was about to ask the people in the church to join him in a song, when, suddenly, the front doors of the church flung open, and the light from the sun shone in so bright that it was almost glaring. The minister shaded his eyes with his hand as the silhouette of a girl appeared in the doorway.

"Sunflower." The small voice of Hilda Yeatts' granddaughter said the name of the girl who had saved her the day before.

Mary stood up and leaned over the balcony to see.

"Sunflower." John Grayling said aloud the name of the girl he had seen at Meeks Feed and Seed store with Daniel.

Milan Reno watched the girl step into the church foyer. "Is Sunflower your name, young lady?" he asked.

Sunflower looked at the faces of the children and the young people. She walked into the sanctuary and looked up into the balcony. "I could not wear your shoes, Mary," she said.

Mary smiled behind her cupped fingers.

"Who are you?" demanded an elderly woman sitting in a chair beneath a stained-glass depiction of Jesus. It was the same woman Sunflower had heard complimenting the flowers in the churchyard. The girl looked at the woman and saw the colors of her spirit. "It is easy to see the color of a flower. But can you see the colors in those people sitting beside you?" she asked.

The old woman could not answer. The question was beyond her comprehension.

"I am Sunflower." She looked first at Reverend Reno and then at the astonished faces around her.

"She's the girl who charmed the snake over at the Corner Store," Sammy Goode's wife spoke up. Sammy was not with his wife. "Sammy said she saved that little girl." Paula Goode pointed across the sanctuary at Betsy, who was sitting next to her grandmother.

"She did save our little girl," Hilda Yeatts agreed.

Sunflower smiled as she looked around her. "I am not a snake charmer. Betsy had faith in my confidence, and she listened to me."

The older members of the congregation murmured. Sunflower could feel their suspicion of her.

"What about Bucky Scaggs?" A woman stood up and spoke accusingly. "Word is you caused him to go blind yesterday."

John Grayling stood up. "Bucky's fine. He can see. I was there, and you people just don't…."

Sunflower raised her hand toward John and stopped him. "His sin blinded him."

"Who are you to be saying someone's sin blinded them?" The elderly woman called from her seat below the stained-glass window.

"She's my friend," a voice called out.

The congregation became silent as all eyes focused on Mary Taylor.

Mary looked at the people around her and then out in the sanctuary. She straightened her shoulders. "You all must listen to her. Don't be afraid. She was brought here by one you all know and love. One who has never harmed a soul in his life."

Mary's reassuring words had a calming effect on the people, and when Daniel walked in and stood beside Sunflower, they sensed his peacefulness with the girl.

Sunflower looked at the minister. "It is true, Milan, that your youthful dream was prophetic. And through your faith, you have breathed life into it. You cannot imagine the souls you have guided by your dedication. Trust me and close your eyes, Milan." Sunflower looked around at the faces of the young and old. She looked up into the balcony. "All of you close your eyes." Sunflower waited until every eye was closed. "Long ago, Milan Reno prayed, not for himself but for the souls of the children. He prayed that through their faith in God, hope would light the paths of their future. His prayer was answered, and he listened and acted upon it." Sunflower touched Daniel's arm. "Likewise there is one here among you who, in his silence, has felt the weight of the world and prayed that the word of God would find its place in the hearts of men everywhere. Though his words were simple, his prayer was for humanity to regain the light of hope in a world gone dark with despair. The answer to Daniel's prayer came in a dream he was not afraid to follow. It was a dream where hope grew from the seeds of his faith. The light of his heart was reflected in a field of sunflowers, sown by guiltless hands and matured by faith. That is where I came from. A place of light, where hope shines with the brilliance of a thousand suns. It is the hope of the world that I offer, but you must know that the words I bring are not mine, but those of my Father.

"Milan and Daniel are not alone, and neither am I. For it is through the faith of ones such as these that we come into the world and walk among you with the truth.

"Now, open your eyes and see the light and color that surround you."

When Milan Reno opened his eyes, he saw again the truth of his dream. The light that filled the sanctuary brought many of the people to their knees. Colors drifted out from their bodies. Colors they could see and interpret. It was as if the people who had lived together all their lives were seeing each other for the first time.

Butterflies came through the front door of the church. The beautiful winged ones followed the laughter of the children and skipped through the light that filled the sanctuary. No one had ever seen such a sight or felt the freedom it afforded them.

When finally the church was filled with colors beyond explanation, Sunflower waved her hand, and the light began to subdue. Soon the bright and vivid colors faded but did not disappear completely from the eyes of the true believers.

Tears of joy streaked down the aged face of Milan

Reno. He was not alone. Hearts were elated, spirits were renewed. Children gathered around Sunflower. With her hands outstretched, she touched their heads, and with her heart, she gleaned the sparkles of life in their eyes. "Bring them in, Daniel," she said. "Bring them, so that all here will see the truth of your dream."

Daniel turned and made his way through the crowd.

"Listen to me," Sunflower raised her voice so that those in the balcony could hear. "The sign in the church yard says that the coming of the Lord is near. It asks if you are ready. But I tell you this. It has begun. The world is changing as you breathe. With every beat of your heart, you are nearer to unity in the light of God. As the world changes around you, be strong in spirit. Feed your faith with unselfish prayers. And seek the light of God. For in that light is the hope of man."

Daniel reentered the church carrying bulging sacks tied with twine. Some of the children who had followed him outside also returned with more bundles.

Sunflower waited until all of the bundles were brought into the sanctuary. Then she nodded, and Daniel opened one, reached in and offered her a flower from his field. Sunflower took the flower and raised it up. She looked at Mary. "There is a beautiful legend told that if one sleeps with a sunflower under his pillow, he will know the truth." Sunflower's eyes fell upon the faces of the children. "Listen to me, children," she said, "for a legend such as this is not without a foundation." She held up the face of the stunning flower. "Look at the round shape of the sunflower and see the world. Look at the seeds and see the true believers who dwell there. And look at the golden petals and know that they are the light of love." Sunflower handed the flower to a little boy standing next to her. "Take it," she urged. "Sleep with it and know the truth of Daniel's dream for the world."

Milan Reno watched as Daniel and the children handed out the sunflowers. As the reverend's eyes fell upon a page in his open Bible, two lines from a parable captured the moment. *The field is the world*, he whispered, *the good seeds are the children of the kingdom.*

That day, no one went home without a sunflower. No one.

Long before daybreak the next morning, a peck at Daniel's bedroom window aroused him from sleep. He opened his eyes.

"Come with me, Daniel." Sunflower's voice was just above a whisper.

Daniel rolled out of bed and dressed as a whippoorwill called from the glen. Daniel heard the squeak of the swing chain and knew that Isaac was there.

Daniel's white cotton shirt felt good against his skin as he closed the door behind him and stepped out onto the patio.

Sunflower was waiting at the end of the pathway near the pear tree.

Daniel reached under the patio table and pulled out a flower sack he had emptied at the church the day before. The bag was filled and tied at the top. Despite its bulk, Daniel hoisted it over his shoulder and carried it as though he were a peddler. "There are no shoes," he said when he came to Sunflower. The girl looked down at her bare feet. "Isaac brought shoes and left them at the edge of the field." The girl started across the driveway.

Daniel walked beside her. "I want to go with you." Daniel felt compelled to say what he did. He knew the world was a dangerous place.

"Yes," Sunflower replied. "But then, what would your grandmother do without you? What about Rita, and Rosie, and all the children in Hopeful who look to you as a symbol of what is right in this world?"

Daniel hung his head. "I am just me." His tone was humble and a little sad. There were so many things he wished he could do. So many words he wished he could say.

Sunflower knew his heart. She stopped at the edge of the flower field. "Oh, Daniel," she began, "if you could only realize the importance of your life to those who come to know you, then you would see that your lack of words and the restrictions of your mind and body have only empowered your heart and soul. The light of God is bright within you. And it shines outward, so that you speak beyond words. Your life is an inspiration to all." Sunflower looked down for a silent moment, until Daniel touched her cheek with his fingers. When she looked up, her tears glistened like diamonds in her eyes. She held his hand to her face and spoke softly. "I cry for the brokenhearted, for the lost souls and the children who suffer in this world. But I will not cry for you, Daniel. I will not, for in the compassion of your heart is the essence of God's love for mankind."

A silence came over the field and the woods. The tiny tree frogs and the ones that burrowed in the cool mud of the pond became quiet. The whippoorwill in the glen ceased its calling. A breeze moved over the great sunflowers and rustled the leaves of their thick stalks. A light began to appear at the center of the field where Daniel had planted his chosen seeds.

"I must go now," Sunflower said.

Daniel opened the bundle he had brought with him. He laid the clothing for eleven messengers beside the shoes Isaac had left at the edge of the field. "Will you be all right?" he asked.

Sunflower touched his shoulder with her hand. "Do not worry, my good and gentle friend. My journey will be long, but when it is over, I will leave as I came." She looked toward the house. "Tell your grandmother that her beloved tends the rose garden that awaits her arrival. And Rita should know already that the heart of Billy Meeks is a gift to her and her child."

Daniel nodded his head and swallowed. "Will I see you again?"

Sunflower smiled. "Yes. When the Son comes again into the field. I will be there to take your hand."

The girl embraced him. "Sow the hills with sunflowers, Daniel," she said softly. "For the rest of your days, live in the light of the hope you have summoned and stay strong in your faith."

Daniel let go and watched as the girl of his dream disappeared into the shadows of the great flowers. And when the light in the field became that of a thousand suns, he fell to his knees and bowed his head.

Return to the Cedar Swing

By the time Isaac Heartwell had finished his story, the sun was falling toward the western hills. A lone dove cooed from its solemn perch among the shadowed branches of the old pear tree at the edge of the garden.

Cassidy Meeks closed her eyes and listened. "The little angel of peace," she said softly. She opened her eyes and looked at Isaac. "Daniel has always said that it is the angel of peace that looks over his garden and comforts him with its gentle voice."

"Daniel is wise," Isaac answered. "He sees the beauty around him and cherishes it."

Cassidy stood up and looked around at the fields of golden sunflowers.

Isaac removed the straw hat from his head and joined her.

"All of this came from his dream." Cassidy studied Isaac's eyes as she spoke. "A dream born from a prayer. He summoned them, Sunflower and the others."

Isaac rubbed his fingers through his white hair and placed his hat back on his head. "Yes. The messengers came through the dreams of those who had not lost hope. They came through people like Daniel, in places all over the world like Hopeful. And then they were sent among men by the Son of Man."

Cassidy put her fingers to her mouth and spoke through trembling lips. "The light in the field." A tear coursed down her cheek.

"Yes, Cassidy." Isaac's voice was as gentle as the expression on his face. "The Son came into the field."

Daniel was still sitting in his chair at the window when Cassidy entered his room. When he heard the floorboards creak beneath her weight, he opened his eyes and smiled at her. "It's a diamond day, Cass." His voice was weak yet joyful.

Cassidy sat down in the chair next to him and held his hand in hers. "Yes, Daniel," she said, "it is a diamond day."

The dove cooed from the pear tree. It was a fitting sound that brought comfort to them both.

Later that night as Daniel lay resting, his body suddenly felt light. Visions of his life passed through his mind like wind-swept clouds. His heartbeat became distant. Familiar and reassuring voices came before the faces of those he had known and loved. Years fell away like seeds from his hand, until he stood again at the edge of his flower field and watched as the girl of his long-ago dream walked out of the light and made good her promise. Daniel smiled and reached out to her. "Sunflower," he whispered. It was the last word that passed his lips, in this world.

*Behold, I send you forth as sheep in the midst of wolves:
Be ye therefore wise as serpents, and harmless as doves.*
Matthew 10:16

Titles by Francis Eugene Wood

The Wooden Bell (A Christmas Story)
The Legend of Chadega and the Weeping Tree
Wind Dancer's Flute
The Crystal Rose
The Angel Carver
The Fodder Milo Stories
The Nipkins (Trilogy)
Snowflake (A Christmas Story)
The SnowPeople
Return to Winterville
Winterville Forever
Autumn's Reunion (A Story of Thanksgiving)
The Teardrop Fiddle
Two Tales and a Pipe Dream
The Christmas Letter
Tackle Box Memories
Moonglow
Sunflower

These books are available through the author's
Website: www.tipofthemoon.com
Email address: fewwords@moonstar.com

Write to:
Tip-of-the-Moon Publishing Company
175 Crescent Road
Farmville, Virginia 23901

Sunflower is the twentieth publication by Virginia author Francis Eugene Wood through Tip-of-the-Moon Publishing Company, which he owns and operates with his wife, Chris. The award-winning author is known for his imaginative and descriptive writing and for his ability to blend the people and places he knows into his stories. He lives with his wife and son in a cabin in the woods in Buckingham County.